MW01137312

<u>The Hustled and Gotten</u>

Joe Evola

Copyright © 2019 Joe Evola

All rights reserved.

A special thanks to...

Mark O'Brien and the Saint Louis pool community,

and, of course, Louie Roberts for the pool room

memories

passed on from

generation to generation.

1

Off to the side in a corner, a middle-aged gentleman stood perfectly upright in a crowded pool room. He gazed into the room acutely observant of the scene before him and took mental notes. He was gauging the pool room, contemplating his next move. He was able to see multiple games played out at once. He wanted to understand, at a certain level, the differing levels of play and of course the betting as it was happening among the crowd of pool junkies. He had a particular player picked out in his mind that he referred to as his "mark." This was the player he would prey on and attempt to take for all his cash. He looked the perfect age, somewhere between 21 and 25 years old, and played at just the level to be hustled by someone like Jasper. A thin, white smoke trail from the edge of the cigarette wedged between his lips drifted upwards and then dissipated into the low ceiling. The smoke found its way through a ventilation system and into the smoke-eaters above. Jasper Slovansky crushed the cigarette into the ashtray by the window.

A pool player loosely held the butt end of his cue stick, and moved his wrist back and forth vigorously, repeatedly. Again and again. Until boom. The colorful, opulent balls broke with a loud thud when the player lunged forward, rising up above the pool table. A pool player was on almost every table. The tables were all nine feet in length and four and a half feet wide, and much bigger than a common bar table. The cloth on the tables was a mild green. The players exchanged cash until sunrise. Just moments later the table was vacated, and then, more players came hustling through the doorway and into the room. The walls of the room were decorated with pictures of old legends of the game, like Louie Roberts and Efren Reyes.

The old bar cues that hung on the walls above the bulky leather seats where the players sat were very old but in decent shape, good enough to be used. There were also signs that displayed humorous, ironic things like "No Gambling Allowed" or "Shoot at your own risk." Of course, gambling on and playing pool was all anyone ever did there. The year was 2006.

If there was a game that most players took a liking to in this pool room, it had to have been 9-ball. 9-ball in particular is very much about hand-eye coordination and natural ability. 9-ball is an advanced rotation game, so you have to shoot the balls in numerical order, 1 through 15. You have to be very guileful in crafting your shape or position for the following shot since you don't decide what balls to shoot; the table layout dictates the order of your shots, which makes your path predetermined in 9-ball. The player to sink the 9-ball in wins the game.

Jasper was in deep admiration of one of the players for how they were breaking the balls. In 9-ball, watching a player's opening break executed properly is like watching an eagle spread its wings for the first time, or a butterfly emerging from a cocoon. To appreciate it fully, you have to watch it very closely and notice the minute details of where the balls are going and how they spin after the impact, or where the 1-ball ends up, whether it is on the rail or out in the open.

Jasper Slovansky noticed something peculiar in that room and it wasn't any of the players shooting or the sound of the balls breaking. It wasn't the smokiness or the handicapped pool room attendant in a wheelchair with his eyes closed. It was the sound of his own thoughts about money. Money was what he saw when he looked at a sucker who couldn't shoot a lick and didn't know how to hold a cue. Money was what Jasper saw when he got down on the cue ball to hit it and his opponent standing next to the table was already shaking in his shoes at the mere sight of him. Money was money. And when you could play, you could play. It was that simple. Money was the source of all his affections and secret desires.

He indulged to money, but at the same time, he wanted it to be about the thrill of the chase. His heart and his soul were all about making the money, hustling for it night and day. Jasper was one of the more audacious gamblers in the country, placing bets on everything under the sun, from pool action to skipping rocks. The thrill kept him going, but the money charged him. Jasper simply got turned on to that kind of bold, risk-taking existence, especially when it was based on his favorite game: pocket billiards.

The next morning, the birds outside chirped incessantly as the summer breeze hit the window to a young boy's room. His mother woke him up from bed. It was early morning. The sky was crystal blue. He grabbed his toothbrush after jumping out of bed and fiercely rubbed his teeth back and forth while counting 30 seconds. That was the rule his mother had taught him. The boy got dressed up in his school shorts, ate breakfast with Mom, and left the house.

As the sunlight hit the pavement, the young boy walked fiercely in his mother's hand. The boy was only 13 years old. It was the first day of 7th grade for little Valentine. His mother, middle aged and attractive, with long blonde hair and sky-blue eyes walked slowly but confidently. She was excited for her beloved son. He was moving up in school and getting good grades. Things were going great in life for them both.

The mother held his hand firmly and said to him, "Son, I have a great feeling about this school year." Valentine looked up at her and replied, "Yes, Mom… Mom, when can I start driving myself to school?"

His mother, Mrs. Madonna, laughed and said, "When you get your license, son. I think you have quite a few years until then." The two of them eventually came to a stop near the bus stop. The bright yellow school bus pulled up right next to them after only a few more minutes as Val could hear the other school children talking among themselves in various sections. Shortly thereafter, Val kissed his mother and hopped in. Val found his seat next to one of his friends. The school bus door closed shut and drove off.

Val looked over his shoulder and noticed a small white building right where the bus had picked him up. It aroused his curiosity immediately. The inside was very dark, but he could see what looked like a bunch of rectangular tables with green on top. The tables were covered up by a heavy, thick cloth for protection. The last time Val had experienced that kind of feeling was on their way to Florida for a family vacation. Mom was thrilled to be going to see the ocean, but when they passed an amusement park, Val's stomach dropped and his ears turned strawberry red. He hated that feeling, because he wanted to be somewhere that he wasn't. But that was exactly how he felt seeing that pool room. He had played that game before he thought, but where? *And what was it called?*

Jasper drove a black Ford Focus. It was nighttime, and this was his second trip to that room in Saint Louis with that funny name: The Number One Hole in the Wall Pool Room. It was where you could find just about any pool player. The evening fog hit the pavement as Jasper made it to the parking lot of the pool room. Jasper was from across the river in a small town in Illinois. Saint Louis was a pretty happening place to be in the pool scene. The area attracted some of the nation's top shooters. Jasper got out of the Focus with a beer in one hand and his cue case in another. The room was nearly empty tonight except for a few locals shooting around. He took in a gulp of beer while scanning the scene before him.

A loud voice from the corner uttered, "Hello, sir, aren't you the gentleman from last night?"

"Yes, I was in last night..." Jasper replied.

"What can I do for you?" he asked.

Jasper, taking another gulp of that Budweiser said, "I'm Jasper, and I hear they got a wild animal in this pool room and they only let 'em out when somebody wants to gamble!"

Big Slick, the owner in the wheelchair, said, "My name's Big Slick, at least that's what everyone around here calls me. And I am the proud owner of The Number One Hole in the Wall Pool Room. Now, who is it you were wanting to play a game with?"

Jasper looked delighted by the question as his eyes lit up at the magnificent charm of the scene before him. A few locals shot him a glance as he gazed in awe at the pool room. He recognized a few of them from around, and a few looked unfamiliar to him.

"Well, actually, would you know someone who would want to bet some?"

The old man in the wheelchair looked around while Jasper stared back at him. Jasper hadn't any idea what to expect to get in response. The question just flowed off his tongue that night, but as it came out, he wasn't sure if it felt so proper. The owner then looked back at Jasper beaming...

The next morning at the Madonna residence, young Valentine was an only child but he always had good friends. Val's father had dated Mrs. Madonna years ago but passed away shortly after. The rest was nothing short of an obscure mystery. Val just hadn't mustered the courage to inquire about it any further. It was a difficult subject for them both.

Valentine and his mother were eating breakfast at the house. He was eating Life cereal in milk with chopped bananas in the mix too. That was how Valentine liked his cereal, with the bananas in it. His mother was eating Cheerios in milk.

"Mom, I saw something really cool the other day on the way to school."

"What was that, son?"

"I saw a pool room, yep... that's what the kids at school called it."

"And you think that's cool, eh?"

"Mom, can I go to the pool room today after school and play there? I promise I'll be back for bedtime."

Young Valentine begged and begged and gave his mother his best puppy dog face until she finally responded with, "No babe, you're too young yet. Plus, you have homework to do."

Val screamed back, pouting and upset.

His mother continued with her lecture, "Babe, you listen to your mother and good things will happen. Good things happen to good kids."

Val said, "Okay, well can I just go and watch the players shoot?"

"I don't like the idea, son, but do as you please. Make sure you get your homework finished, and don't go over there alone. Bring a friend."

Little Valentine's mother was a very good woman and always knew what was best for her son. She always looked out for Val.

A few hours later, Valentine was sitting at his desk in reading class. He was doodling on a scratch piece of paper while the teacher spoke about the class reading. The girl next to him couldn't stop staring at what Val was drawing. It was a doodle of a pool player holding a cue like a rifle but the player was wearing a cape pretending to be a superhero.

The teacher, at the front of class lecturing the students noticed what Val was doing in time. The girl sitting next to Val named Lucy whispered over at him, "Pay attention to the teacher! Don't you like to read?"

Once Val was in too deep with the doodle, Mr. Moore stopped talking.

The teacher finally said, "Val, what is that your doing? It better pertain to the subject of the reading or we are going to have a talk in the hall…" Embarrassed like he had never been before, Valentine blushed and remained silent. He looked down at his doodle like nothing major had happened.

The teacher continued, "Can you please bring it up here and show me what you have there? I'd like to see what the rest of the class has to say about it."

The kids in the classroom stared as Val walked up to the front of the room with his head down. The teacher took the piece of paper and looked at it.

Mister Moore said, "Aha, very intriguing. Billiards, huh?" The class saw it and started bawling as the teacher shook his head in disgust. Val's face was bright red. The teacher continued, "Get back to your seat, and start paying better attention, please."

Val acknowledged this and did as he was told.

The teacher continued, "Now based on the reading, who is the hero in this story?"

Val wanted to raise his hand to answer, but he realized he didn't have any idea what the actual answer was since he had been too busy working on his doodle. Lucy raised her hand, eager to answer.

2

After school was out, Valentine felt that it was time to see what this game was all about. The fact that he was among the youngest in the pool crowd just inspired him to be great. It drove him to want to be something bigger, better than a young student. He honestly didn't know any better at the time. The boy could hear the balls clashing behind the door to the pool room, the cues hitting the floor, and the players making hefty wagers as he stopped and collected his thoughts.

Valentine noticed the little sign above the door,"The Number One Hole in the Wall Pool Room." Valentine sort of thought that was funny. His sense of humor was very mature for his age, as he saw the humor in this because most pool room owners don't like to be seen as just holes in the wall. Hole in the wall, Valentine recognized, was slang for a "dive bar."

Young Valentine walked into the pool room with his head and spirits held pretty high. When he first had stepped foot inside, he felt like Neil Armstrong landing on the moon, not quite knowing what to expect entirely. Valentine was welcomed by a cloud of smoke as he stepped inside. He noticed a bald, elderly man sitting in a wheelchair at the counter and walked over to him.

"I'd like to play pool."

"Son, pick up a cue and have at it."

Valentine looked down like he was pondering something.

"But Mom says I shouldn't play, and I'm too young."

The man in the wheelchair replied, "Son, you are welcome to play pool here as long as you follow the rules, see the sign?"

Valentine looked over at the black and white sign next to the counter, "NO GAMBLING, NO WHINING."

It was in that very instant that Valentine was absolutely hooked on something for the first time in his life. Valentine knew it the moment he saw that ridiculously stupid sign. It was one of those aha moments that made him laugh and think at the same time. He couldn't wait to pick up a cue and try it out.

As the owner of the establishment, Big Slick, just chuckled quietly to himself, Valentine raced over to the wall where a bunch of rusty old bar cues hung. He found a cue that he liked and analyzed it. He stroked it back and forth with his hands until he found one that was a comfortable weight and size for him. His hands were smaller than most, so he had to be choosy. He felt very intrigued and inspired just touching a cue for the first time in his life.

It was truly an awe-inspiring moment for Valentine because he had honestly never seen so much activity like this before among adults. He almost felt out of place because of how young he was compared to the oldest person in the room. But he would soon get used to that. For now he was one of the few players who couldn't make two balls in a row.

A tall, African American man was shooting over on the main table next to the entrance while Val watched him from a distance. The man was middle-aged and looked like he would probably be one of the best players in the room by the way he stood next to the table with perfect posture and stance, feet correctly positioned so that his body was prepared to stroke the ball with most accuracy. He had a necklace around his neck that swung like a pendulum over the table when he got down on a ball. A small crowd was observing him. He was running racks in a crowd of predominantly Caucasian males.

Then, the man saw Val watching him. He shot the white-colored boy a glance and grinned. The tall, dark-skinned male, like a tiger hunting its prey, stopped shooting suddenly when he saw Valentine. The man then proceeded to walk towards Val and started talking to him.

"Aren't you a little young to be here. You do know where you are, don't ya?"

Valentine looked intimidated, but remained calm and poised.

The man laughed a little, reached out his hand and said, "I'm Deon. And you are?"

"Valentine. I'm from across the street."

Deon said, "And what's a little boy from across the street doing in a place like this? You do know this is a betting parlor?" Valentine looked startled and confused and replied, "I thought it was a pool room?"

Deon giggled and replied, "It certainly is!! But people also bet money here. I just don't see a lot of boys here. You looked kind of lost."

Val ignored his last comment and started hitting balls with the stick. He miscued often but still had a lot of fun. Deon eventually resumed his business as usual. Being in that pool room that night and observing everything around him was like watching the whole world go round. The competitiveness of the shooters matched with Val's own curiosity about what was going to happen next, and to top it off the special attention this shooter that approached him was getting when he played pool, was all plenty to swallow. Even for some of the players who didn't shoot or go there much, it wasn't hard for them to get enthralled in some of the action of the pool room.

Valentine danced around the big table, trying to shoot balls into the big table pockets, missing most of his shots, but enjoying the hell out of it. Val then paid the man at the desk five dollars for an hour.

Big Slick said smiling, "Did you have fun young man?"

Little Val nodded his head and left.

The next morning, little Valentine woke up. His eyes had big bags under them as he looked in the mirror and handled the toothbrush. He started brushing his teeth. As he brushed, his reflection in the mirror changed and his teeth turned yellow and his face got longer and longer as he thought about pool and the betting parlor that he had visited last evening. *Was this just his imagination?* He saw his mother in the kitchen making breakfast. He had to confess.

His mother didn't speak to him yet.

Little Valentine looked up at his mother and said, "I went to the pool room last night, Mom."

His mother frowned and said, "Son, what did I tell you about pool rooms being for older crowds? Well, was it fun?"

Val replied excitedly, "It was awesome! I got to play for five bucks and I shot real good, too! Can I do it again tomorrow?"

His mother blushed and said, "As long as you don't get yourself in trouble. And remember the buddy system? Please do not go alone anymore. Bring a friend with you!"

The wheels turned inside Val's head like a merry-go-round. He was more than excited to hear these words out of his mother's mouth, and he knew exactly who would want to tag along with him this time. He jumped up in his place and smiled. This almost brought a happy tear to his mother's eyes, as she noticed how anxious he was.

Later that evening, Val grabbed one of his buddies named Marty. Marty was a little shorter and stubbier than Valentine, but had a pretty good head on his shoulders for his age. And Valentine knew his mother would appreciate that.

Valentine said to Marty, "Marty, I have got to show you something."

Marty replied, "What, Val?"

"It's a pool room across the street from my house. The school bus will take us there. Do you want to come? It will be fun!"

"Sure, why not?"

Inside the pool room, Valentine and Marty talked casually about the new place they were at. It was pretty new to Marty, but Valentine could tell that Marty was enjoying it by the way he smiled as he held his bar cue. Marty even expressed interest in getting his own cue stick someday. For the time being, he enjoyed the house cue. Valentine and Marty were playing 8-ball, as that was the only game that they knew. Val and Marty had learned it by playing online games on MiniClip.com.

There was an intense match going on between Jasper, an up--and-comer with a shady reputation and a nickname, and a big time money player, Deon Williams. Deon won most of his bets and hardly ever lost money when betting on his own pool playing expertise.

Deon said to Jasper, "Whatchya gonna do for a buck or two, Misery Man?"

The various people inside the pool room became interested in the betting and people started making side bets while the action ensued. Valentine and Marty looked anxious and a little desperate to see something happen. They decided to lie back and observe.

Deon and Jasper were playing 9-ball. The bet had quickly escalated to a thousand dollars a game. The boy observed and found the way these guys were playing it simply beautiful. Valentine's eyes lit up as he watched them battle it out taking turns running balls.

Deon was shooting now. He was making a lot of balls in succession; ball after ball dropped into the pocket. And then, he ducked playing a defensive shot. This confused Valentine a little as he watched. But eventually he realized what a safety shot was.

Jasper was shooting now and he managed to kick and get a good hit on the ball ending up relatively safe.

"Alright, alright. So, you're ahead by five thousand. What do ya say we play for it all? One set for all of it? Race to seven!"

Deon and his crowd from the Lou got a real kick out of this, and a few people may have even laughed. This was insanely brave of Jasper. Deon replied confidently, walking over to the jukebox, "Bring it on, man."

Deon played Muddy Water's "Hoochie Coochie Man" on the jukebox and then walked slowly back over to the table, but with a beam of intimidation. Deon was just the kind of player who knew how to make a man tick. This put the fear in Jasper already, and it got under his skin. He felt like the whole world was crashing down on him when this song played for some reason. The audience, the smoke, the music, whatever it was, it was in his head now.

Jasper got down on his ball. It was the 9-ball, little Val could see. The money ball. The ball to win it. The score was six to four, Deon's way. Deon was on the hill. Jasper needed two more games to make it hill-hill. Jasper got down on the cue ball and stroked it. The ball jarred in the corner pocket.

Deon giggled, "Weak sauce, man. You were just teasin' that time."

Jasper cried, "Ya know it's funny, cause mind over body, I'm supposed to make that ball. Mind over body every time."

Deon got down and won the set, sinking the 9-ball. Jasper threw his cue on the table and looked down into his dirty wallet for the cash he now owed Deon.

"Do you ever miss? I just don't believe this guy... You never miss do you, bro? You had so many chances to miss a ball that would have cost you the game, and you never missed one ball!"

Deon said, "Haha, Misery Man. You've done it this time. You're losing it, man. What you think you are, special? Pay up!"

Jasper reached into this wallet and sifted through his money, counting the twenty-dollar bills. He threw 1,000 dollars on the table. Deon's jaws dropped after he picked up the money to count it.

Deon said, "There's only one thousand bucks here, man? Come on, where's the rest?"Jasper looked at him with a sad, puppy-dog look on his face. At this time, little Valentine walked discreetly outside the pool room with Marty, and they watched from outside.

Marty said to Valentine, "What's going on with these guys? Don't they have jobs?"

Valentine shrugged.

Val and Marty decided not to leave yet. They could barely make out the dialogue between the two gamblers. Everyone had left the room except for the two players. Deon's buddies were outside now too, talking at a low volume.

Inside the room, Deon said, "You still owe me nineK. So, that's all you got, huh?"

Jasper remained quiet as a church mouse.

For the first time since he had been in the pool room, Valentine experienced doubt. His palms began to get sweaty as he glanced over at Marty with uncertainty. Maybe this wasn't such a good idea? But then, he heard the other spectators talking, whispering and it got his attention.

Andy, one of the observers and a close buddy of Deon's spoke to Bobby like they were tough guys.

Andy said, "That Jasper, man, he's really got another thing coming if he don't got the chili this time."

Bobby chimed in, "You mean he's done that before? Not had the money?"

Andy retorted, "Yeah, ya can't renege on your bets in this game. That's how money players get a bad name."

"If he don't got it, what we gonna do?"

"Use your imagination!"

Deon and his buddies walked into the pool room again to listen in on what was happening between the two players.

Deon said, "Is this a joke? A prank?"

Deon and his boys looked ticked off. Jasper tried to calm them down and said, "Look, I'll get the rest of the money, Deon. Let me just go get my credit card out of the car."

Jasper slowly backed up and left the room while a couple of the guys snickered.

Deon Williams whispered over to Andy, "Andy, go check to make sure he's not ditching us!"

Andy went outside to look for Jasper. And much to his shock and amusement, Jasper was nowhere in sight. It was desolate, with nobody around except for little Valentine standing a few feet away from Marty. Andy noticed Val as he was standing outside next to the pool room.

"Hey, kid, have you seen a guy walking around out here? He's kinda short, skinny with brown hair?"

Val and Marty shook their heads and played dumb. They wanted to stay out of this mess that Jasper was in. As Valentine and Marty walked towards home, Andy dashed back into the pool room and yelled.

"He ran away!" Andy shouted.

"Fuck," Deon said, and everyone ran outside to look for him.

Jasper was hiding high up in a tree while they searched everywhere for him.

Deon said to Andy, "Hey, Andy, is this his car? The Focus?"

Andy replied, "Yeah, yeah, that's the one I saw him in earlier when he pulled up."

Deon instructed Andy to help him with the tires, as they began to sabotage his vehicle, slashing the tires until it was inoperable.

Jasper stayed perfectly silent high up in the tree still. Sweat poured down his cheeks. Jasper watched as they cut his tires with the blades. Jasper felt personally victimized now, like he was the culprit. *How did he let this happen?* He hung high in the tree. Jasper ran out on his tab! Fortunately, though, he remained physically safe from the people below him.

Deon and his boys all drove off in separate vehicles. As soon as they sped off, Jasper tried to shimmy himself downward, but his leg caught hold of a branch and he quite clumsily slipped and fell flat on his back. On the way down, his head hit a few of the limbs and got bloodied. Jasper had bruises all over his body and his face was bleeding from the fall. He had been knocked unconscious. While Val returned safely to his home, Jasper lay there in the grass directly under the tree in the middle of the night.

3

Valentine was no longer little. As he had grown into a young adult, things had really changed quickly for him. Pool and billiards took a backseat and he was now managing a rental car shop in Saint Louis, MO called Borrow for Less Rent a Car. Val Madonna was twenty-three years old. His buddy Marty Kyle, who he went to school with, also happened to work out of the same office location as he did. There was not a cloud in the sky and the temperature was a comfortable warm.

A blonde gentleman looking to rent a vehicle came in to the office. He was going on a business trip he had explained rather bluntly.

"Yes sir, and what kind are you looking for? We are all booked out of sports cars at the moment, but on the pro side we have just about every other kind of car you may be looking for."

The man looked more than satisfied and said, "I noticed you had a Town and Country on the lot out there. Can I have something like that?"

Val replied, "Absolutely. Let me get some information from you first. Could I get your first name, please?"

Marty was at the cubicle beside the front desk overhearing the conversation play out. Marty knew Val and their business was struggling and wanted to ensure every customer was treated right. Marty had received a warning from corporate that he and Val needed to produce more. Sales were falling, and the business as a whole wasn't doing so well. Marty was very worried.

The customer at the front desk said, "Darren is my first name. Last name, Thompson."

Val typed the name into the computer, verifying the spelling. The line to check out rentals got very long and the other clients started to get impatient with him. Marty had to stop what he was doing and get up to help. Since a few other workers were out sick that day, it was getting hard to keep up.

One of the customers in line complained, "This place is a joke! The line is outside the building now and you only have two workers at the desk? Gimme a break!"

Val walked his customer out to the parking lot where they hopped in the Chrysler for routine inspection of the vehicle.

"So this is our Town and Country Chrysler, great for long trips and such. It's great on gas mileage. And quite frankly, sir, I think you are just going to love it till death," Val explained, sounding more and more eager for the commission he would be getting for selling the insurance.

"Wow... well I better drive carefully then, huh?"

Darren decided to fake interest and contentment. He proceeded with, "So, how much will this vehicle cost per day again?"

Val replied, "It will come out to exactly thirty-five dollars a day."

Darren inquired, "What about gas?"

"You have to bring the car back with the tank at least three quarters full."

"Okay, okay. I'll be renting for the whole weekend. Let's wrap this thing up!"

Val finally got him settled into the Town and Country and they parted ways for now. He then made his way back inside to find the next customer.

It was Friday. After work, the night grew dark. Val, along with Marty and Lucy decided to go to the pool room to hang out and have a drink. And, of course, to shoot some pool. Little Valentine had a hobby in the works since he was thirteen. Ten years can really change you, but Val was still a junky. He was desperate to get into some action, but at the same time had to support his girlfriend.

Val made most of the money. The money was like a catalyst in their relationship. Already moved out and away from his mother, Valentine had a good life with Lucy. Now, Lucy and Val were tight. But they were not married. Val simply hadn't muscled up the courage to propose yet, but would like to someday, Val thought, and they talked about it on occasion. It just wasn't the time yet. Very young still, they were going to have to wait a while for that. Lucy was a computer person. She worked in a bookstore part time. She had blonde hair with a ponytail and walked with a sort of country groove that made a lot of older men look twice. Lucy stood six-feet tall, and she looked very mature for her age.

Marty, being the overly aggressive, attention-seeking type in the pool room, decided to run his mouth and call people out to gamble. He skipped and hopped around the room asking pretty much everyone there to play him for money.

"Hey, sir, you wanna play for some money?"

The stranger replied, "I ain't no good."

Marty looked over at the guy standing next to him and asked, "Hey, YOU want to play for some cash?"

Marty looked pumped up, turning to the next guy, "I'll play anybody in here for even money!"

The next stranger giggled and said, "Want to flip a coin? Hehe, I'm no good either."

Marty raised his tone a little and said, "Gee where's the action?"

Lucy caught wind of what Marty was doing and walked over to him. She said, "Marty, you're fooling yourself. Just play for play. Come over here. Play with Val and me."

Val and Lucy just wanted to have some fun with Marty. They didn't want to see him lose any money or get into any trouble. And in that pool room, there was plenty of opportunity to do just that.

The bar owner heard about Marty running his mouth in his pool room and got a little excited. His name was Kenny and he played pool like he was angrier than a mule. In fact, that was his deep, dark secret he tried to keep from his opponents. When he was angry he could shoot the lights out. Kenny was a stout guy with grey hair and a little goatee. He always dressed casual even though he was the owner. He did an excellent job with making customers feel like family, but when someone in his pool room acted the fool like Marty, he was usually there to stop him dead in his tracks.

Kenny walked over to their side of the room and approached Marty in a hurry.

Kenny said to him, "I'll play you some!"

Marty replied, "What you want to do?"

"Hang on a minute. I'll be right back."

Marty looked very confused holding his pool cue standing there next to the table with Val and Lucy. But when the owner made his way back to the table where they were shooting, Val and Lucy sat down nervously.

Marty's face lit up like a strawberry after the owner came over to him.

"I'm Kenny, and I own this place. I'll play you ten bucks a rack with this broomstick!"

Marty broke down laughing hysterically and could hardly control himself. He then took a minute to respond and finally agreed, "Alright. You can have the first break!"

Marty, chuckling pompously, lost his ass to this guy very quickly. But little did Marty know, and much to his dismay, Kenny had his broomstick sharpened to form the shape of a pool cue at the end of it. And he shot sporty with that broomstick, too.

It was four games in a row and it was all over but the crying. Val and Lucy sat there giggling watching while this was all going down.

Marty handed him the forty bucks and said, "Here ya go."

Kenny gave him a look of understanding, a smirk and then looked at the money. A pause ensued.

Kenny handed him the cash back and looked Marty straight between the eyes, "You can keep it."

"Wait, are you sure?"

Kenny was just too good of an owner. Val almost had to woof at him he was such a good guy. But quickly, Val learned that would have been unwise. Woofing was the art of asking somebody to gamble.

Marty and Kenny stood there next to the table while Kenny explained, "Yeah, I'm sure. I'm sure that you learned a lesson. I don't take money from my customers unless it's for whiskey, food, or pool time. Got that?"

Marty, embarrassed like never before, almost decided to take up a new hobby. He walked over to Lucy and Val.

"Kenny can shoot a lick, huh, Marty?" Lucy jabbed.

"More than a lick, shit!" Marty replied.

Val finally chimed in to the conversation with, "Sure can! Marty, you look like you just seen a ghost, man. Literally, bro. I mean how do you lose to a guy with a broomstick?" They laughed together at this.

Kenny walked back to the bar and resumed his business. Marty claimed it had a tip on the end of it, but the people watching seemed too focused on the brush at the other end.

While Marty took a quick hiatus, Val was off to having a great night with his girlfriend, Lucy. Val was just the kind of person that when he even cracked a smile, he lit up the room with his dimples. The girls fell for him like he was Elvis or something, and they simply went gaga over his wardrobe. There really is something to be said about a sharply dressed man, and Val was the embodiment of that concept wearing a slick, red-collared,short-sleeved shirt and cargo pants. Not to mention, he was on fire that night shooting balls in like it was going out of style. He had taken his game up a notch lately. His focus was more powerful than ever before. This was going to be a special night, he thought to himself.

His gal, Lucy, sat there observing him. They exchanged glances quite often as the hours went by and talked a little here and there, too.

"I finally got the misses out of my cue, babe. I haven't missed a ball in almost eight hours straight!"

Val was, at the time, completely indestructible on the table. He was like the king of that pool room.

Another hour went by, and he barked, "I'm a straight-talkin,' smooth-strokin' slayer. Val's my name, and pool is my game!"

Sly Ty, a local, full-fledged authentic professional pool player, walked in the room at this time. He held his cue over his back with his hand stretched over his shoulder, clutching the leather handle with one eye on Val's practicing.

Ty said, "Nice shooting, bro, really nice."

Val looked up from the table after sinking a ball in.

Ty continued, "So what's your name?"

Val walked over to him and replied, "I'm Val. Wait, aren't you Sly Ty, the pro?"

"Yeah, that's me. Well, would you be interested in joining a pool league that I run? I'm looking for some more players, and it looks like you've got some talent there."

Val reached and grabbed a couple balls from the table and rolled them onto the cloth, dodging the question. Val shot the 4-ball into the corner pocket, then made the 5-ball, losing a little shape just so he could bank in the 6-ball casually. He proceeded with the out and then took a deep breath of air, looking Sly Ty square in the face.

While Val talked to Ty, Lucy approached Marty at the other table. She noticed out of the corner of her eye that Sly Ty handed Val a business card. Val took it.

Marty stopped shooting and stood upright.

"I think that guy is a pro player, nicknamed Sly Ty," Marty explained.

"Sounds like they are going to make Val an offer or something."

"No, probably just some league or a bet or something. Yeah, he's a world beater, though."

Lucy took a huge breath and swallowed deeply. She then walked back to the table where Val was playing and making conversation with Ty.

Ty stepped up to the table and racked up a game of 9-ball. Val then reached for his breaking cue, bent over the table, and cracked up the balls. They spread apart quickly, but it was a dry break. In pool, most of the serious players used at least two different types of cues: a break cue and shooting cue. The break cue typically consisted of a tip with a phenolic resin at the end of it, the same material as the cue ball. This maximizes power on the break, so the balls clash and spread out a lot on the table, making it easier to run them out.

"So, what do you think, Val?" Ty asked as he played a safety, hooking Val on a neutral ball. This was a common tactic in 9-ball when a player doesn't have a good shot on the object ball, or an easy chance to make it in a pocket.

Val kicked at the ball, barely getting a good hit on it, leaving Ty a relatively easy run-out. Without breaking a sweat, Ty got up to the table and ran out the rest of the balls.

Ty said, "I like to live my life by this motto: Good things happen to good players. Now, what do you think of playing in the MCSA with me?"

Ty was always looking for an angle, but not the kind you would find on the pool table. No, that kind of angle was too easy for him. Ty was the real deal of pool shooting out of this area. He knew that Val was a cocky youngster who wanted to prove himself. It was Ty's opportunity to help him with that. At least, that was the general idea.

Ty randomly speared a ball in, stroking hard! He then turned up the pressure, "Our next session starts in a couple more weeks. I can reserve you a spot on my team if you want."

Val, very enticed by this, replied, "What's it cost? What about the league fees?"

Ty responded by telling Val that he would cover his fees for the first couple weeks, and that it was under twenty dollars a night.

This was enough to seal the deal for Val, convinced that it would be a great chance for him to break into the pool world.

"So how does this league work? Is it handicapped?"

"Yeah, it is handicapped. And since I've been watching you, you haven't hardly missed a shot! I was thinking we could really make something out of you, and we could go far together."

"Give me some time to think it over with my girl. Lucy? Lucy, this is Ty, he's a league rep for the MCSA, Men's Cue Sports Association."

Ty reached out, offered Lucy a loose handshake, and said, "Nice to meet you, Lucy."

Lucy said, "Likewise. We will discuss this tonight, right, Val?"

Val gave Lucy a kiss on the cheek, and they started smiling, cordially and agreeably. To Ty, this was like getting stood up on a first date, and he could barely stand it. No, in fact, he couldn't stand it. He secretly vowed for revenge if this young up-and-comer didn't want any part of him. On top of it, he was appalled that they wouldn't agree to it yet.

4

Val had always wanted to be a pool player from the moment he stepped into that pool room as a young boy. He had focused on improving, in terms of both mind and body, his pool game for a long time before he was able to run balls like he could. He was dreaming big from the moment he gazed in at the pool players from the school bus on his way to school.

And now, a pro had asked him to join a league with him. It was a life changing opportunity that he wanted to capitalize on. He wanted to take his game to the next level so badly he had almost forgotten his real job at Borrow for Less. Ty claimed that the MCSA had sponsored many pool players to play the game professionally once they reached a certain level of play and won enough pool tournaments. Ty wanted him to join the league badly, and Val wanted to oblige him quickly.

Val and Lucy were sitting on the couch at their apartment discussing the offer. And Lucy didn't seem to be convinced about it. She felt like Ty was putting him under too much pressure, too fast. She thought work took priority here.

Lucy pressed, "I'm just not sold on this one, babe. Joining a pool league like this will distract you from your financial goals. We have bills to pay and debts to pay off still. Can't this wait?"

Val retorted, "Gee, you're a hard sell! Seemed like a pretty cool guy, didn't he? Look, this league and all, I think it's a golden opportunity for me: my one shot at taking my game to a new level. I've always wanted something like this, Lucy!"

Lucy argued, "But isn't this game just a hobby? C'mon Val. You've got a career life ahead of you, and this league is going to distract you from us and your future. Plus, we don't have the money to spend!"

"Listen! I love pool. I'm starting to move better. Running out more and all."

Lucy said, "Yes, I get it. That's true, but still…"

Lucy understood. Yeah, she was a real sweetie, but when it came to men and their billiards she was living in another world. Val loved Lucy, though, of course. It was just a matter of being on the same page and not crossing boundaries.

Val needed a drink.

The following day, Val got out of bed with an eagerness and positive attitude towards life and pool. The pool world had finally engaged him in a way and it had excited him to the fullest extent of his desires.

Val drove a car that the company lent him on a lease program. It was part of the deal of having a full time position. The vehicle he drove for work was a blood-red Nissan Maxima, and Val loved it. It suited his taste perfectly, he thought, as he drove to work. It symbolized his hunger to succeed in life and go for the gold. He was a true go-getter. The car he drove from his work embodied that idea.

In the office, Val blinked repeatedly as he looked into the eyes of the formidable NOM, National Operations Manager. His name was Steve Civy, and he didn't look too pleased with Val's performance at work. Steve kept a level of decency about it, though.

The manager said to him, "Do you understand why we are having this conversation?"

Val did have a clue why, but didn't feel like giving it away quite yet for various reasons.

"Is everything okay?"

Steve responded with subtle laughter and continued what Val thought was a power trip.

"Okay, the primary reason why I called you in today is, well, the overall level of customer service. Also, it has been brought to my attention several complaints from various customers all over the map, Val, of course, involving you."

Val almost died inside himself. This was an awfully vague explanation of something that he didn't want to consider yet. Was he fired? Where was he going with this? Val thought, I'm doomed!

Val replied, "Involving me?"

"Yes, involving you."

Val swallowed hard.

Steve adjusted himself in his seat like he was getting prepared to make the finishing move on Val.

He continued, "You've worked hard for me, Val, but you've been coming in late for work regularly, doing only God knows what on the weekends… and so we have decided to let you go."

Val's stomach dropped, and he knew he had to get the hell out of there. No, not yet, not before he gave Steve a piece of his mind. He clenched his fists tightly and grimaced.

In controlled anger, he replied, "What? You've got to be…"

But before Val could finish his statement, Steve cut him off.

"Please remove yourself from work, effective immediately. You can leave your shirt and tie in the waiting room, as well as the badge. We wish you well, son!"

Son? Who did this guy think he was?

Val looked down and then back up at Steve. He was crushed and devastated by the outcome of this conversation. What would he tell Lucy? Lucy would be furious with him now.

"I'm sorry, now go be on your way."

Val got up out of his seat and left the small office, shutting the door.

Later that day, Deon Williams was getting ready to crash a pool room. He hopped into a taxi cab in Chicago which he intended to take directly to Chi Town Billiards pool room where he knew he could make a killing for the money. This was pool slang for hitting it big and beating everybody and their mother out of their pocket cash. He was an older player from Saint Louis and was already an intimidating household name there. But in Chicago, he was an unknown. It would be like taking candy from a baby.

On the opposite side of that coin, it is sometimes difficult to be on somebody's home table, or be playing out of somebody's home bar.

Just as he exited the cab, paid and tipped the driver, he received a call from an anonymous phone number.

"Hello?"

"Yo, Deon… word on the street is your boy is back in town."

"Man, I'm in Chicago right now, what boy?"

If Deon identified his voice properly, this was Bobby Daffie he was speaking with. Bobby was a long-time friend of Deon's and used to go with him everywhere in the pool scene. But Deon hadn't seen him in years so it wasn't perfectly clear who this was yet.

"That one crazy sumbitch who ran away from us and still owes us 9,000 dollars. I think some little kid was there, and he helped him get away, if I recall correctly."

"Is this my old buddy Bobby who I haven't heard from in years, haha?"

"Yeah, it's Bobby."

Deon squinted, trying to remember and said, "Oh yeah, yeah, that cracker from Illinois named Jasper!"

"He's been dodging us, Deon, and I'd say it is time to collect!"

"Let's meet up at the pool room in two days Bobby. I need some time away for a bit."

Back in Saint Louis, Lucy and Val were emotional about the fact that Val was now jobless. The moment was getting very heated as they exchanged arguments back and forth in the house. Lucy paced around the room shooting Val a glance every once in awhile as they argued. Val just stared back at her, jabbing here and there with his words of comfort. Neither one of them was quite ready for it. The termination caught them both by complete surprise.

"What the hell, Val?"

"It's going to be fine! We're going to be fine!"

"How are we going to pay off our debts now? The car, the mortgage? This is fucked!"

Val looked speechless. He had been let go after only working at Borrow for Less for six months, and now he was forced into a situation with Lucy where he had very little options. It was not fair to him, he thought.

"Just keep cool, we are going to find a way out of this mess. There's other jobs out there! Look, I have a college degree."

"How can I keep cool? This is really bad, Val!"

Lucy took a glass and slammed it over the table.

Lucy continued in anger, exclaiming, "Hon, I don't know what to say to you! What is going to happen? So now it's all up to me to support us? You better find something quick, or I'm gone!"

Val's stomach dropped, and he started to sweat profusely. This could be the end of his relationship with Lucy. But he simply could not give up yet. There were options.

"No, no Lucy, it's not. I'm going to find another job. Something even better than what I had, and we are going to be just fine! Relax!"

Val put his arm around her. It was the best argument he had for her at the time. He tried to console her, to comfort her in the wake of this storm. Lucy deflected Val's arm, and frowning, she started to cry in front of him. Val wouldn't let that happen, so he tried to add some levity to the situation.

"Hey, babe, at least you are due for a promotion at the bookstore," he added only because that is what she had mentioned last week before this volcano had erupted.

Lucy then cracked a genuine smile. They both retired to bed. There would be no sex that night.

At Big Dog Billiards the next day, Val was drinking a Bud Light at the bar with Marty when he noticed a suspicious, yet somewhat familiar-looking, older man out of his peripheral vision. He was shooting pool at the table where Val and Lucy usually played together.

This man had brown hair that looked like it was almost about to turn grey. His physique was narrow but solid looking for the most part. He didn't falter in his movements around the table.

Val finished the beer, tipped the bartender, and walked steadily over to the mysterious gentleman playing pool on his home turf. Now this was truly something, he thought. Why was there someone playing on his court and on his table, that he typically played on? Val was just like that you see. This was his territory. Val proceeded en route to the man at his table slowly and a little awkwardly.

"Excuse me, mister... hey, buddy!" Val said confronting him.

This man had somebody watching him set up what looked like trick shot on the table. It humored Val a little because most of the guys he had heard of that did trick shots were youngsters, with a few exceptions who happened to actually be renowned trick shot champions: Mike Massey and Charlie Darling to name a couple.

Val announced himself near the table, "Hey there, mister, this was my table."

The man finally looked up, noticing Val.

"Was your table, kid. Look, we are betting real money here."

Now Val wanted in on the action. The wheels turned inside of Val's head as he took in the situation and picked apart what was going on before him.

"Now, Freddy, like I said, I can make the 8-ball in any pocket. All you have to do is tell me which one to make it in, and I'll do it in one shot!"

"That's impossible, sir. But go ahead and try!"

"Okay. How much you want to bet on it?"

The man had set up the balls so there were six balls surrounding the 8-ball, three balls on each side, frozen against it. He clutched the cue ball firmly in his grip.

Val stumbled back onto his chair and decided to observe from a fair distance. He was as skeptical as Freddy.

"C'mon, I'll match the bet and we'll put the money in the light here above the table. C'mon Freddy…"

Freddy's hands shook violently. Finally out of his mouth came the words, "Make it five hundred."

Freddy pointed to the side pocket and said, "This side pocket here!"

The old man hesitated, took the cue ball, and placed it near a spot on the table that would allow him to execute the shot. He got down on whitey after he was certain it was lined up properly. The old man stroked whitey and it crashed into the stack of balls. All the balls separated in a hurry as the 8-ball screamed into the side pocket.

He then yelled, "How sweet it is!"

He reached up to grab his cash from the light.

Freddy cried, "Well dang, you proved me wrong, I guess. Have your money! Have your fun!"

The man staggered over to Val now.

"Did I take your table? I'm sorry, I had a point to make!" He was an old timer who could still shoot a lick of pool, even though most cocky youngsters probably thought otherwise. The older pool players were strong.

Val replied, "I'll play a game with you. What do you want to do, grandpa? It looks like 8-ball is clearly your game. Why don't you try me some 8-ball?"

"Kid, does my hair look grey to you? I'm no grandpa, and if you call me that again, you might not make it home with more than a few dollars left in your wallet."

That statement alone was enough to intimidate the youngster. But in the pool room, there were no rules against intimidation. It was simply part of the game. These guys were some real die-hards. They worked hard and played pool harder.

They played 8-ball at twenty dollars a game after a few exchanges back and forth about the terms of the bet. Marty had been observing some of this and feared for his buddy Val, so he came over to try to talk some sense into him.

He said quietly, "Val, what the hell are you doing?"

"I'm getting in some action. Why?"

"Man, you just lost your job! Grow some common sense! What are you doing betting... ? You're out of your damned mind, bro!"

Val sort of shrugged Marty off his back and continued to engage his newfound prey. Marty walked away frustrated and a little scared. Val was in over his head, clearly.

Marty spoke to a few of the other players who stopped to watch the action, "That's Jasper... Jasper Slovansky. He's back in town again..."

Val had had enough talking and decided to equip his Predator breaking cue. Val whacked the stack of balls as hard as he could. They sprout out quickly after a loud thud. It was like a gunshot. Boom!

The break was dry.

Jasper approached the table and grabbed a piece of blue chalk. He chalked up loudly and vigorously, staring Val down as he did it. Val looked right back at him and felt some nostalgia.

Jasper finally got down on the 1-ball and speared it in, while it took no time for the cue ball to deflect off the object ball that it collided with and land ideally for his next shot.

A small crowd of locals appeared before the table, a little too close for comfort maybe, and started to observe the matchup.

While Jasper tried to run the rack out, the locals muttered various things, just barely quiet enough not to disrupt the play.

"Hey, ain't that Missouri Jasper?" Another figure in the crowd claimed, "Oh yeah, yeah....say it ain't so. Thought he was on the road for a while."

"No, no... heard he just got out of the nut house or something."

Val giggled and so did a few other spectators.

And then another figure from the crowd uttered rather loudly, "Hey, Jasper… How much of an allowance did ya lady give ya this week?"

Jasper leaned back and regained his posture.

"I was just getting warmed up…" Jasper said with a stern look on his face. It simply rolled off his tongue. He showed no fear.

Jasper won the first game and then the next. Eventually he found himself up 100 dollars on Val and that was when Val threw in the towel.

"I quit."

Val stood up and walked over to the old man.

"Well, sir, I've gotta admit. You're a real dandy of a shot."

Val looked down at his wallet and frowned. He then looked back at Jasper.

Val said nervously, "What if I didn't have the money?"

Jasper then changed moods. He stepped an inch too close to Val, chest to chest now.

Jasper said, "Don't you say that. Don't you ever say something like that!"

"What's the matter?"

"Look here, kid. A long time ago back in 06' when I was a youngster, I got into it with these guys over at this pool room and…"

Jasper told him the whole story from start to finish and Val's nostalgia from his grade school years grew stronger. He remembered but then again, he did not. It couldn't be. *Was this the man who lost his marbles back in the day and climbed up that tree? Wasn't that the year he first discovered pool?*

5

Jasper woke up from unconsciousness next to a large tree right outside the pool room. He felt the blood oozing out of his nose that was caused by his head hitting the ground below. Bruises all over his body, he got up slowly and finally back on his feet again.

Jasper walked over to his car and there noticed that someone had slashed his tires out so that the car was virtually inoperable. He didn't have a way home.

Home was in Illinois. Where was he? That's right, Saint Louis. Damn. That's a long walk.

"Did they really slash my tires???"

Suddenly, he remembered. He had a cue. *Where was it now? Was the pool room still open?* Jasper rushed inside and attempted to bust the door open but was greeted with the sound of a loud thud and a shoulder burn. The door was locked.

He yelled into the pool room, "Where's my damn cue?"

He had no choice but to do what his grandfather had warned against for so many years. But he had to do it. He was going hitchhiking. Maybe the bruises would help? If he portrayed himself as hurt and victimized, somebody might pick him up out of pure sympathy. Jasper was cracking himself up.

Home was 100 miles away. The walking distance was overwhelming to say the least.

Jasper held his thumb out, looking for a ride. He walked and walked onward towards Illinois. Somebody would come along. Some curious fella would eventually feel sorry for him.

Val, back in the present day, shuffled his last 100 dollar bill for the old man and said, "That was my last one."

"What's your name, kid?"

A moment of silence followed between the two gamblers as they both looked around, realizing the spectators had gone elsewhere. That's when Val knew it was Jasper from ten years ago. He didn't want to bring it up but he knew. He could remember that sleazy, gambling degenerate of a man who threw air.

"Anyway, the point I'm trying to get across to you is don't ever bet without the money."Jasper proceeded on with his narrative, "Val, I like your heart… you play with a lot of that…."

He pointed to Val's stomach. "But, you've still got a lot to learn about pocket billiards. It's a whole new world out there. Inside, you are a real savant waiting to happen…"

Jasper abruptly walked over to the bar to get himself a drink, now disregarding Val. Val followed in hot pursuit of him.

"What are you drinking?"

"A Bud Light. Thanks."

Some players called Jasper "Misery Man" because he threw air a lot in Missouri. At present, Jasper's net worth equaled the amount of cash he had profited from Freddy in addition to a stack of bills he had kept hidden underneath his bed. He had zero, zilch else to live from. His landlord was also getting ready to kick him out of the apartment, not to mention the amount of money he owed to Deon and company. He was in deep trouble with them.

Jasper, in his effort to make money for himself, had attracted some unwanted attention. Deon Williams and his crew had met up at the pool room and while Jasper and Val were talking, Deon was watching them from a distance. Deon was making small talk at the table on the opposite side of the room with a group of people. It was Deon, Bobby, Andy, along with a few girls from across the river who Deon and his boys were swinging with.

Deon, their obvious leader, was a very gentle giant. He just had tough friends that made him appear tougher than he was. On the outside, the guy would never hurt a fly. But that's not to say that he was a softy. He never wanted to be the victim of an air barrel like Jasper. Nope. Not a day in his life would he live that down. Deon was not a pushover type. He would have his way one way or another on that deal. Deon was also a great pool player and action junky. He loved the action and thrived on it. He rarely played a pool tournament. Deon shot a subtle glance over at Jasper, who was discussing things with Val.

Jasper continued to make his impression on Val, roping him in. Val was taking this all in, very convinced that it might be going somewhere. He was ready to enlist in Jasper's army of pool players, or so it seemed.

"When I was playing you in 8-ball, I was studying the way you shoot, the way you stroke the ball, and you've actually got some enormous potential. For the cash, you're a lot better than you think you are. With a little work on your pool game you could really become somebody."

Jasper's pep talk made Val blush a little, but it had his interest right now, of all times. Val seemed a bit skeptical, though, of his so called enormous potential. He inquired further, "What do you mean 'for the cash?' I fucking dogged the set, man."

"I mean from a gambling perspective. Pool ain't all about winning kid."

What kind of angle was this man playing him for? It wasn't an easy one to understand at the time, but Val kept on persisting.

He changed the subject, "You by any chance heard of the league MCSA? It's new around here, and this guy Ty approached me about it and I... "

Jasper quickly interrupted, "Listen here, kiddo, leagues are fun, they're cool, but if you want to make some real cash, hustling is where it is at!"

Val suddenly dropped all thoughts of joining the league. His brain was being pulled one direction and then another. He couldn't help but be a little uneasy.

"Okay, alright," Val uttered submissively. He literally felt obligated to trust Jasper, not just because he was cool. Val could remember him from the story he told, and it rang a bell inside of Val's memory. It just clicked inside his brain that Jasper could be the answer to what he needed out of life.

"Here, you see this cue stick? It's a Terbrock cue. My great grandpa gifted it to me when I was a young wise crack like yourself."

"Woah. Very cool!"

Jasper continued, "He passed along to me a great deal of wisdom, the same kinda wisdom I'd like to pass along to you."

"Let me guess, you're going to give me the Terbrock cue stick now?"

"Hell no, kiddo, I'm going to teach you how to run. You see, pool is a mind game. It takes place up here, in your head. If you can get your head around every shot and visualize the path, you've already won half the battle. Pretend every shot is like the bottom of the ninth of the World Series. If you don't get your footing and posture right and you don't stroke the ball properly, the ball is already in the catcher's glove, kid, and you've lost the game."

Val liked that analogy and pretty much consumed every word that came out of Jasper's mouth. Val liked Jasper from the start. They were going to be good friends, he thought.

"You look like you could use a road buddy, kid. You ever wanted to just play pool, make a bunch of money, and not have to work ever? Look, pool used to be the coolest thing that ever hit the block, and people everywhere wanted to either play it or watch it live on television. Back in the early nineties, pool was unbelievably popular. Nowadays, you're lucky to get even decent action if you walk into a pool room with a Facebook or a Twitter account to your face."

Val understood this man very well and heard him loud and clear. And he was correct. With technology nowadays, hustling pool was next to impossible. People could communicate easier with cell phones and cameras on them. If a player was getting a big name in your area, anyone who was anyone would know about it eventually. He saw the next question coming like a bat out of hell. Jasper paused briefly, letting his words sink in for Val.

"So kid, I have to ask. Are you on Facebook, Twitter, let me guess you have a Myspace account? C'mon, spill the beans, kid."

Val shrugged and said, "I'm not big on Facebook or Twitter or Myspace. The only thing I have is a LinkedIn profile."

Jasper's expression went from solemn to happy, and he smiled vaguely. What Jasper just realized about Val made him one of the most eager and excitable people on the planet. He now had loads of energy built up and was ready to take this kid for on-the-road pool hustling. Val had no idea what he was in for. *Who was Jasper, anyway?*

"I heard you are out of a job," Jasper said adjusting himself in his seat like he was getting ready to depart from the bar. Jasper then continued, "Let's meet up here tomorrow, okay? Here's my card."

Jasper handed him a white business card that contained a picture of a 9-ball on it. It had Jasper's name on it and it read, "call me for birthday parties, weddings, and splendid evenings." And below that it said Trick Shot Artist. Val got the goosebumps at the mere sight of this goofy business card. The man had to have been a little bit daft. But Val liked him. It was a funny feeling for him.

Jasper leaned the glass beer in his grip towards Val and their beers clinked together.

"Let's make some money!"

Deon took the crew to the bar. He bought the girls food and treated them all like princesses. They didn't want to make a stink out of a pool bet in front of the ladies, so Deon decided to just scope out Jasper for a while. After the girls went home, it was just Deon and Andy left at the pool room.

Deon spoke first and said, "We need to find a way to get our money. Nobody pulls a fast one on me and then tries to embarrass Freddy. Man, did you see the way Freddy cried after what that sicko did to him? That ball ain't supposed to go in that easy. That was insane, man!"

Andy replied, "Yeah I'm with you. How much did he take off Freddy?"

Deon, "Look, man, it don't matter. Now that the old man is back, we are going to wait for the perfect opportunity to get OUR money, what belongs to us!"

6

Val had only dabbled once or twice in his lifetime with the idea that he could play pool for money. He was thrilled someone was going to do something for him but at the same time he was a little nervous. He was about to get involved in the pool scene, he thought to himself. And whether that was pool league, or gambling on pool, he was going full throttle, full speed ahead.

Jasper had him figured out to the bone and wasn't going to miss the opportunity presented to him. Val was vulnerable to Jasper, and Jasper wasn't afraid to manipulate and control him. He had seniority over the youngster, and everybody watching them play the past evening knew it, too.

Val was at home on the couch watching television all day. He flipped through the different channels. ESPN 2 was one of his favorite channels to watch. He loved the singles sports like tennis and billiards and just about anything involving one-on-one competition.

Billiards was playing on ESPN 2 and it immediately grabbed his interest. Justin Bergman was playing doubles with his partner Sky Woodward. They were facing Jayson Shaw and Darren Appleton, two well known legends from Team Europe. Europe had not lost this competition in years and Team USA was getting frustrated with this.

The Americans played the Europeans in the Mosconi Cup Tournament, considered the intense version of golf's Ryder Cup. It involved four days of world class pool from each team's top five players. Val loved watching this every year. It was everything he dreamt about and more. The Mosconi Cup was among the most dramatic events in the billiards world for professional pool players. It started in 1994 and it featured six men and two women. Nowadays it is just the male players.

Later that night, Jasper took the wheel and picked Val up from his house. Jasper now drove a black sedan, a Chrysler. He sold the Focus years ago after the tires were slashed.

That day was the beginning of the end of Val's life as an ordinary, working-class man, struggling to keep a 9-to-5 job. Val was going to turn over a new leaf.

Before long, the dark colored Chrysler pulled up in Val's driveway, and Jasper honked once. Val heard it and got out of the house faster than a five year old gets out of bed on Christmas morning. Val was eager to start something new. He had high hopes for himself and that this might just be the ticket.

They started driving along on their way to Big Dog Billiards Bar And Grill, the same pool room where they had met the second time.

"So tell me, Jasper... What do you do for a living?"

"Let me answer that by telling you about my past. I grew up without a lot of free money and education. I had to sort of hustle my way through life. I hustled a lot to make money, okay? I mean, you heard my story about me being up in that tree, didn't you? Well I want you to learn something from me about life and money, okay? Not everyone has it made in the fucking shade, kid."

Val said, "So, you were a roadie? A pool hustler?"

"I was and am, but you see pool is dead without youngsters like you who can grow and learn. With young guys like you, our sport has hope. Pool is not dead, kid."

Val looked intrigued, raising his eyebrows, and added with a bit of excitement, "So I'm pool's hope?"

"You're going to be a big part of it. If you want to be."

"Look, kid, I practically grew up sleeping on a pool table and living underneath one. We are what I like to call 'thoroughbreds.' We stayed away from leagues, kept our head down on whitey, and laid real low, and I mean real low until we found a mark. Then we went after 'em and got their money."

They finally pulled up to the pool room and parked in a remote spot away from the other vehicles.

"Okay, thoroughbreds, huh? I've already been bred, though. And why not play pool leagues? That guy Sly Ty says it could help take my game to the next level."

"Yes, I know what he probably said to you, Val. The truth is, leagues are just out to get in your pocket. We're going to keep you under the radar for a while and I'll teach you some tricks. Some hustles that will make you and me both money."

"So what are you trying to say, exactly?"

Jasper chuckled and said, "Have you ever even watched a pro stroke the cue ball? They've got that follow-through, that perfect stroke when you seen it over and over again; it's like you just saw it for the first time, every time you see it. You know what I mean by that, kid?"

His talk was getting Val pumped up.

Jasper continued, "That's the kinda stroke I want you to have…. That kinda thunder, that intimidating factor."

Val took a deep breath of air. Jasper rolled down the window after bombing another cigarette.

"Kid, I want exactly what you want, okay? But just remember, sometimes ya got to go through hell to get to Heaven. This game isn't easy, but under my wing we can team up on the pool scene. Pool is hard, kid!"

Jasper closed the window back up, when shortly after he heard a loud thud on the glass window. They both jumped in their seats and turned to the left.

Jasper rolled the window back down again and peeked outside the vehicle to see Joshua, Jasper's old road buddy. Josh was about as old as Jasper, and wore a long sleeve shirt that had the logo, "Chasing the Dream" on it. Joshua had a reputation for looking out for people in the pool scene, particularly players who were considered underdogs. Jasper fit into a different category.

"Jasper! You've gotta watch out. I heard there's a player lookin' for ya named Deon. He's got a crew of guys on the hunt for you, man."

"I owe them some money from a long time ago, but I can't afford to just blow away nine thousand dollars. I got a new road buddy..." he said, winking at Val.

"Look, I'd like to help you get out of this mess, but I'm in between jobs and I just can't. I hope you guys figure it out, I really do."

Jasper nodded and agreed. They needed to be careful. Joshua and Jasper reminisced for a minute, and that was it. Joshua went on his way. Jasper had been warned now. Maybe this would be his second chance at redemption. *Why didn't he just pay those guys off now while he could?* Val had learned from overhearing the conversation between Jasper and Josh that Jasper was about to get evicted for not paying his rent. His landlord, Jason, was hot on his toes about getting him out of the apartment he was staying in. Jasper didn't have anywhere else to live, but he knew things were going to get ugly in due time.

Val and Jasper exited the vehicle and began their walk towards their local room of choice. The sky was a clear blue. Fall weather was approaching. The wind was starting to pick up, as it violently found its way through Jasper's thick hair. Val's short hair trim stood strong in the breeze as they walked through the lot.

Val was beginning to pick up on the way things were going. He was getting used to being Jasper's friend and tool at the same time, but didn't want to really argue with him about it because most of the things Jasper told him seemed true and believable. He really was a lot younger than Jasper. The old man was right. Val grew more and more curious about the act of throwing air as he hung around with Jasper. *Why did people do that? Did it happen often? And why was this man who had done it helping him out so much? Did he have a conscience? Did he have any sense of right versus wrong? Was one supposed to have a conscience or was that not proper in the betting world?* Val was at odds about certain things.

Inside the room, Lucy and Marty were hanging out at the local pool room talking. Marty ordered a nice, juicy cheeseburger for himself at the bar. He asked Lucy if she wanted anything. She politely refused.

"We need to find your boyfriend another job, and fast."

"No shit, Sherlock."

"I heard him and that old timer might be going on the road. We're going to have to talk him out of this, Lucy!"

Marty feared for his buddy Val. He feared for Val's life more than he did his own right now. He thought at least Lucy was on his side.

Ty Dino walked into the room. Sly Ty, the same character who asked Val to join his pool league, had opened the door and walked in when a few other locals noticed him right away and greeted him near the entrance. He had his cue case behind his back like he meant business. Ty took no names on the pool table. Ty walked up to the table next to where Lucy and Marty were talking and playing aroundt.

Ty started running racks casually. This was nothing but typical for him. His pump strokes in midair matched with a degree of confidence that stood out to most spectators were enough to humble even the most knowledgeable of players.

In pool, there was an element of knowledge and skill and if you had both you were in good shape. The amount of knowledge involved in the game was overwhelming at times for common barroom players. But for professionals, it was just a matter of pulling certain information from your brain and equipping it, utilizing the knowledge when it mattered most.

Ty Dino had a lot of skill and an average level of knowledge, some would say. So he was a weaker pro. But having just been assigned league operator of the MCSA, his confidence was at an all-time peak.

A few minutes later, Val walked in with Jasper right behind him. They stormed in right behind Ty.

"Hey, Lucy."

"Hey, Val, and you must be Val's new friend Jasper." Lucy scrutinized Jasper. Then she continued, "I saw you guys playing pool the other night. So who wound up winning?"

Lucy didn't seem too pleased to meet Jasper.

"I'm Jasper. Nice to meet you Lucy. I only beat him out of a few bones. I'm teaching him how to run!" Jasper extended a hand for Lucy as he introduced himself.

Ty was looking over their shoulder from the other table and eavesdropping on their conversation. He stopped shooting.

"Oh yeah, you know how to run alright!" Ty yelled over them.

Marty stood there and laughed at Sly Ty in the background.

Ty was being a sarcastic little jerk. Being a pro, he had inside information into all the gamblers, both bad and good, that were out there. Betting on your expertise was a big part of being at the top level, or any level of pool. Pool and gambling were very much like brother and sister. They related to each other, but were not exactly one and the same.

At Big Dog's, you could hear Eric Clapton playing out of the jukebox. The bartender cranked up the volume. She must have been a fan of Clapton. The song was ']"I Shot the Sheriff," one of Val's all-time favorite Clapton songs that was originated by Bob Marley.

Val ignored Sly Ty's interjection and so did everyone else. He obviously knew something about Jasper's history.

Val set his cue case against the table and walked towards the bathroom, clutching Lucy. Val looked a little upset.

"What's the matter now?"

"You do know why he is here don't you?"

"No. To ask you to play league?"

"Yes! Look, I really can't play league anymore. I am making other plans!"

"So.... Just tell him no."

"Lucy... arghhh... you don't get it. The guy is a professional!"

Lucy nodded her head in agreement. She was just Val's boyfriend. She was playing her part and doing a superior job of it, too. Val did appreciate this, but his voice failed to show it.

Suddenly, a voice cracked from behind them as they hid away from the group. It was Ty's voice.

"So, my friend, did you think it over? My offer?"

"Yeah, I'm out man. I just can't do it."

"Are you for real? Hmmm… I thought you'd be all over it. The opportunities you're missing out on…"

Jasper, after grabbing a drink from the bar, quickly noticed the way this was playing out and he didn't go for it at all. He looked out for Val now.

"No more chit chat, kid," Jasper whispered confidently. "So like we talked about, keep them LPs out of the mix!"

LPs was short for League Players, and Jasper was clearly insulting Ty with this. Ty could hear him loud and clear, too, despite Jasper's attempt at discretion.

"You sicko! Don't you know who that guy is? He's a pro!"

"Of course I know the kid…"

"That kid's a champ! Asshole."

"Look, I'm a good asshole. Just stay away from him, okay?"

Val didn't always go for this kind of drama, but he knew the difference between Jasper and a pro. Jasper was one thing, and a pro another, that was for certain. The real question was, are hustlers also professionals, just under cover from the scene?

"Get your cue stick out. I'm going to tell you something that's going to help you out with your 9-ball game."

Val did as he was told. He unzipped the cover from the cue case and pulled out his cue. He played with a Meucci cue. It was custom made.

"There are exactly fifty-four different ways to shoot the cue ball. Now, let me explain…" Jasper instructed him.

Jasper took out his Terbrock cue and did a few pump strokes, explaining his philosophy about 9-ball.

"You don't have to tell me how to play this game… I…"

Jasper quickly interrupted and retorted, "Kid, I've been playing this game since before you were riding in a school bus, so get used to it."

Jasper set his cue stick on the table and inched closer to Val.

"I'm going to train you so the hair on your opponent's arms will stand up when you get down on whitey. Now get down on the cue ball."

Val did as he was instructed. He got down on the cue ball. Jasper noticed his left foot was not planted properly. Val, being right-handed, had his left foot parallel to his right, which was not technically proper mechanics. Jasper corrected him.

"Point your left foot in line with the shot, like this." Jasper demonstrated the technique. Jasper also taught him how to keep his back straight and butt out. He taught Val perfect posture on the table. Jasper said that this would really put the fear in your opponents from the start.

"Once they see you know how to stand properly on a table and hold the cue right, they're going to fold in their seats, kid."

Val already knew how to make balls and thought that Jasper was just humoring him. But with what Jasper was teaching him, he could make them under the kind of high-stakes pressure that they were heading for.

"Now, run 'em out, Valentine. Snap that wrist!"

Val broke the balls. A loud thud. He attempted to make every ball, executing his shots and getting shape perfectly on each post. He made the 9-ball straight in, then another, banking the 9-ball in this time. Swish!

"Stroke of genius. Beautiful thing!"

After that, he taught Val how to break properly and how the technique used when breaking in 9-ball was different from other kinds of breaks. Jasper advised him to snap his wrist like you were going to draw the ball, but not to aim too low as to cause whitey to scratch in the corner pocket by the kitchen. You wanted the cue ball to come to rest around the middle of the table.

Jasper also explained how the break in 9-ball is about speed and finesse, not power.

Jasper liked Val's stroke, and Val knew it. They were getting smarter together. We're going to be a good team, Val thought to himself. They were going to be indestructible and a force to be reckoned with.

7

Lucy was at the bookstore working. She had a big stack of books in her hands as Marty strolled through the building, looking for her. Marty tracked her down in the store to tell her the news about Val. Marty wasn't sure Lucy was getting the big picture, so he had to talk to her.

"What's going on, Marty? Why are you out of breath?"

"It's about your boyfriend, Lucy. I think he went on the road with Jasper. We need to talk."

"Let's talk tomorrow. Call me!"

Marty decided to leave it at that and left. He didn't want to interrupt her while she worked. Marty knew more about road players, particularly Jasper, then did Lucy. Marty knew they got into trouble a lot, and he knew that Jasper was one of those types. Road playing was dangerous and always had been. It was considered very risky practice. And Jasper was a living testament to that.

Jasper and Val were finally on the road together. They were on a mission. Their destination was a pool room in Illinois closer to where Jasper grew up. There was sure to be plenty of gambling going on in this place.

They pulled up to the pool room in their car after a long, forty-five minute drive that felt more like twenty minutes to Val because it was a scenic route. They had the pleasure of seeing the Saint Louis Arch from a distance, speeding through the outskirts of town.

"Okay... kiddo," Jasper said rubbing his hands together in the driver's seat. "I bet you've never been here before, have you? This is Sharpshooters."

Val agreed that he hadn't.

Jasper continued, "There's bound to be a ton of action in here... and some money to be made for sure. Like we talked about, just follow my lead."

They both got out and walked, still talking. Val asked him, "What's the game plan? Are you putting me in?"

"No, I'm just going to expect you to win. And if you end up losing I'm hitting the road."

Val looked confused and ticked, "What the fuck?"

Jasper looked serious for a minute and then said, "You're a real piece of work. Yes, I am backing you. Can't you take a joke? Let's get the ball rollin.'"

Jasper held the door for Val. It was his time to shine, to light up the pool scene.

After they got inside, Jasper and Val stopped dead in their tracks at the sight before them. It was truly something else what they saw in their midst. It was like a scene straight out of the movies, and Jasper could barely remain calm and composed. His hands shook violently as he gripped his cue case in anticipation.

"You just walked into a place where everybody only cares about two things, kid: Your cue and the size of your bankroll."

Val laughed and said, "What is this: a strip club or a pool room? Well, you better have a bankroll, then, because you know I don't!"

Jasper and Val walked up to the counter and asked for a rack of balls. They found an open table and started playing, hitting the balls around for amusement.

It was not long before Jasper commented about one of the players that he noticed in the room. The guy was tall, a little bit husky, with brown hair. He dressed like he had a nickname too. His black-and-white T-shirt that said Cue Sports on the front of it stood out conspicuously.

Jasper said to Val, "Hey, look who is in the room. Fast Joey. Kid, go over there and woof at him like a hungry pig. Ask for weight, ask for the world playing 9-ball, 100 bucks a rack. Go ahead, make him think you mean business."

"How do you know this guy? He any good?"

"I've known Joey Fast since I was your age. He's good, but I think with a little weight you could take him for everything he's got and the car keys. Just remember, if it goes back and forth a lot, just shoot back at him, and he'll buckle. They always do when you fight back, trust me."

It was the first time Jasper had ever tried to make Val money getting him in an action game. Val was thrilled. He wasn't nervous at all. The way Jasper spoke to him it just wasn't that big a deal, win or lose. So he really wasn't that nervous. But at the same time he didn't have a clue what to expect.

Val walked over to Joey and asked him to gamble. Joey pulled his jeans up and looked him between the eyes. Fast Joey was not really a known player nationwide but he had quite a bit of popularity locally. Joey looked cocky and wasn't afraid to be dressed pretty flashy, too, like a young gun on his way, but he didn't seem quite that young, either.

Joey replied, "Action? What do you want to do?"

Val did just as Jasper instructed and demanded, "Give me the last four and the breaks!"

Fast Joey almost killed himself laughing and said, "I'm not giving you weight. I don't even know you!"

Val quickly got creative on his feet and said, "I heard you were a pretty damn good shooter, so I just thought I should ask. I mean, doesn't that sound fair to you?"

"Okay, who did you hear this from? I ain't nobody, but what were you wanting to play? 9-ball, 8-ball?

"9-ball and hundred bucks a rack."

"For that amount of money, you're going to have to adjust a little. Plus, like I said, I'm no pro. How about I give you the wild eight. Take it or leave it."

Val felt like he had just hit a home run and tried to control the feelings inside of him that told him it was going to be insanely fun to beat the pants off this cocky kid. He held his man and looked away for a minute.

Fast Joey and Val battled for a while. Jasper stood firm, observing the action take place. Cues waved around vigorously. First Val hit the ball, then Joey stroked the ball, both trying desperately to get a leg up on the other.

Part of the gamble was a game of muscle, a competition between two strong players involving a great deal of perseverance and fortitude. With such a clash, it was all a matter of breaking the balls good. And when both players broke well, all that mattered was the one breaking. But on this particular nine-foot Diamond table, the cloth was worn out, and Val was not used to playing on it yet. So it wasn't exactly going to be run-out city at Sharpshooters.

Fast Joey knew the table all too well, because, of course, it was his territory to begin with. Val had approached Joey so it was only customary for them to play on his table. Fast Joey must not have seen this coming because he was missing balls often and rubbing his hair after each miss. However, at the same time, he wasn't the house pro here, either. He was just a player rumored to have a dangerous cue and a high level of play.

The game continued to go back and forth, back and forth. 9-ball after 9-ball was potted.

The tables had turned. And they had turned in Val's favor this time. Val started spearing every ball he looked at and didn't miss anything. The weight had finally taken its toll on Joey. Val had made so many balls consecutively that if he had made one more he'd be too hot to trot without feeling the heat on him. He knew something wasn't right from the way that Joey was looking at him. Joey looked like he wanted Val's throat. It wasn't long before he was up a few hundred bucks on Fast Joey. And then another hundred. Another and another.

Val got up 1,000 bucks before Fast Joey finally said uncle.

"Man, I don't know if I like this game," he said, unfolding ten hundred-dollar bills and handing them to Val.

Val took the money from Fast Joey, but wasn't sure how he felt about it. He had never taken that much money from another person before. His badass rating just skyrocketed, and his pool-playing ego was at an all-time high.

Val received his winnings and went to show Jasper.

"Now, do you understand the theory behind what we did here?"

Val sighed and shrugged. He wasn't sure what Jasper wanted him to say.

Jasper took a puff of smoke and looked the other way, and then put his arm over Val. He whispered softly into the youngster's ear, "Always, always ask for more than you need. Always. Hasn't anyone ever taught you this?"

"No. But isn't that a hustle?"

"Look kid, it's like being a salesman… it's a business, okay?"

Val persisted this time, "No… that's hustling… I know it is. Jasper, is this right?"

"Not when your opponent is a known… you see you gotta be humble in this game. So now next time you match up with him, you'll still own him."

Val was still unconvinced and felt brutally dishonest inside. But he did what he had to do. Val looked around for Joey and didn't see him anywhere. His insides were hurting, though. His conscience was knocking him around inside. He was going to have to get used to it. Together, they had asked for a ridiculous spot that Jasper had known full well Val didn't need. It was a bad game for Joey.

"Well, Val, I think we just woke up the lion's friends, and they don't look too happy."

Fast Joey wasn't the kind of person you wanted to try to hustle. Fast Joey was talking with some of his buddies on the side and pointing his finger over at Jasper and Val, when shortly after, a few of them started casually walking over to him. One of them was enormous, and cracked his knuckles while staring them both down intensely. Val turned around.

Lucy and Val had been friends since grade school and started dating seriously when they both turned sixteen years old, at which point they had already passed third base together. She was about through with him, though. And that alone was very shocking, but at the same time justified. She was livid. Val had let her down to the core this time. And now Marty was trying to convince her not to put the fire out.

Marty was at Val's house talking to Lucy, assessing the situation.

"Lucy, what did Val say before he left this morning?"

"He was taking on a new job."

Marty was speechless. Did Val seriously say this? It was horrible. The worst. Val had transformed to the dark side completely and betrayed Lucy.

Marty replied, trying to analyze the problem correctly and appropriately, "This is not good. Well, what did you say in response? I mean we both know that comment to be a little deceptive in nature. Taking on a new job could mean multiple things. But from what we know he went on the road with Jasper, hustling pool for a living. Fuck, Lucy, I'm not sure what to do."

Teary-eyed, she said, "I'm just about done with him. If he comes home with a black eye, I am through for good!"

"Well, look… all you have to know is it's not actually possible to hustle people nowadays. With the internet and technology, it's going to be next to impossible. So we don't have to worry about him. What's the worst that could happen?"

Marty tried to comfort her. Marty was always a good friend, looking out for everybody in his circle.

"You're right, Marty. Anyone who sees him shoot like he does can just take a picture of him and post it online, right? Not to mention cell phones nowadays…"

"Exactly," Marty agreed. Hustling was a thing of the past. They both agreed on that. Or did they? Lucy looked a little skeptical still. Marty wasn't going to give up, though.

Back in the pool room with Val, Jasper, Fast Joey and gang, the front door was blocked by a massively obese gentleman and Val had no way out, now. He turned to Jasper and…. Jasper?

Jasper was nowhere in sight, now. Val scanned the room, quickly checking his peripherals and all. He had vanished from the pool room. *Where had Jasper gone?*

It was just Val, Joey, and Joey's henchman now. This was going to be trouble. Val dashed over to the bathroom and shut the door. He then locked the door.

He started to panic. Then he noticed there was a window above the stall. Someone was knocking on the door very loudly. The window to the outside was just barely large enough for him to fit through. He stood on the bathroom seat and pried open the glass window. It wouldn't open, so he propped his butt against the wall enclosure for the stall and started kicking the window, until it eventually cracked open and fell off onto the grass below.

He could hear someone was pounding on the door still. Boom, boom!

Somebody yelled into the bathroom, "Kid, you better have a good excuse for this! We don't tolerate hustlers around here!"

Val shimmied himself out the bathroom window head first and landed awkwardly in the grass below. Mostly unscathed, Val looked around for Jasper's vehicle.

Suddenly, his black sedan appeared out of nowhere.

"C'mon, get in."

They both sped off in the car at 100 miles an hour.

"Why'd you disappear all of a sudden?" asked Val.

"What, you think I'm going to let this get out of hand? Those guys were the wrong crowd for us, kid. Not everyone is going to take kindly to hustling around here. Let's find some action elsewhere."

"Where we going, Jasper?"

"There's some cheap pool tournaments downtown in Saint Louis this weekend. I'll pick you up, same time tomorrow."

Jasper had this all mapped out accordingly so that they could make money, and they had. They had already scored once. Now it was time to see what tomorrow would bring.

Jasper drove Val back to his house. He said his goodbyes and reminded him to be ready to go tomorrow.

"Get a good night's sleep, kid."

Val slammed the car door shut. He walked up to his front door and entered the house. Lucy was already out for the night. Val retired to bed shortly after he got home. But before he drifted off, he lay in bed, dreaming next to Lucy. He snuggled up with her and ran his fingers through her blonde hair. Inside, all he could think about laying in bed that night was his next big score and what that would entail. *How much would he win, and who would he play? He also reflected on his failing relationship with Lucy. Could he win her over doing what he was doing now?*

Sly Ty was at home on his home table. He was doing drills, getting ready for a big tournament coming up, an amateur tournament that the state of Missouri held every year for the best of the best. The kicker was you had to be a Missouri resident. Ty was a three-time champion, but this year was different in that the pros were putting him under more and more pressure. He hadn't won any pro tournaments in at least a month and he was starting to worry. He was also considering playing in a tournament in Las Vegas.

Ty was just furious that Val rejected his offer. He had to get revenge somehow. He had a cute girl, Ty thought to himself.

Ty speared another ball in harder this time and did a few more air pumps before the next shot in the drill. Ty had also heard about Val's road playing with Jasper through one of his contacts. He knew Val was on the road now and wanted to take a shot at Lucy. Lucy was perfect for him. Ty already had what he wanted in the pool world: prestige, status, skill, money... He had no sympathy for Val after the embarrassment he had put him through. The league was suffering, and if they didn't get more players soon, Ty might lose part of his income from MCSA Corporate.

8

The next day, Lucy and Val hardly spoke to each other about anything of substance. They both had their own agendas and needed some space. Val was waiting patiently for Jasper to come over so they could start their day together.

Jasper picked him up again from the house.

While the two boys discussed their interdependent strategy for making money, Lucy was just getting to work. Her day went by slowly and painfully as there was very little work to do that day. She finally clocked out at 4 PM and left the bookstore.

After Lucy got off work, she stopped in at the bar for a drink. She ordered one shot and a Tequila for herself.

Her mood was very somber. She had not felt this melancholy ever before, and wasn't exactly sure what to think of the situation with Val. She didn't want to see him lose his job, but he did. And now he was undertaking a very risky practice to make money. *Was it going to work?* She should have just told him to join the pool league. That would have been a better scenario.

She heard a cat call, a whistling amid the bar. She turned her head and saw Ty, the pro player. She nearly jumped in her seat.

"You must be tired, honey, because you've been running around in my head all night," Ty said to her, grinning stupidly. Lucy nearly spilled her drink on him.

"What?" she blurted out.

"Hey, I don't know if you remember me, but I'm Ty Dino, the league rep from the MCSA. And your name is … remind me again, please?"

Lucy wasn't taken by flirtatious men very easily and nearly got up and left right then, but something about Val being gone made her change her mind, or maybe it was the Tequila.

"I'm Lucy. Lucy Morgan."

"Pleasure to meet you again, and that is a beautiful name I must say…"

Lucy blushed and smiled at the same time.

"Yes, and what can I help you with, Ty?"

"I just wanted to talk," Ty explained simply as he inched closer.

"I heard your boyfriend went on the road with that Jasper character, and I thought you might want to talk to someone who has had that kind of experience. You do know I'm a pro pool player, I would assume?"

Lucy did. So she agreed and nodded her head.

Ty continued, "So… with my status in the pool scene, I have to, you know look out for some of the younger amateur players that I see. Your boyfriend is running around like a little rascal. Hell of a pool player, but he needs to realize times have really changed. Hustling is not an easy way to make a living anymore. Before long, the other players are going to be able to identify him. Cell phones make it easy."

"So… what do you want me to do about it?"

Ty sat down next to her and ordered a drink for himself. Lucy was already a little tipsy. Her cheeks were flushed and she was slurring a little in her words.

"I don't expect you to do anything about his hustling. He'll learn his lesson eventually. I realize you might think leagues are all competitive and serious, but there's a fun side, too. We're not all heavy weights and gunslingers, you know? Sure, leagues have their share of hot shots, but they also have a few who know how to loosen up and have some fun. Hey, mind if I share a story with you about league? It happened the other day… funny stuff here."

Ty was playing his cards really close to his chest tonight. He was dead serious but at the same time trying to loosen her up a bit, soften her up for the final blow. Ty's intentions were hard to identify sometimes. He didn't like to be an open book.

Lucy replied after taking a gulp, "Are you trying to sway me into joining your league now, too?"

Boy, you must be dreaming, Lucy thought. Ty continued to push his luck. She didn't want to bust his chops, though.

"Lucy, I want what is best for you."

Ty was getting more serious now. He reached in and rubbed her leg gently. If she weren't drunk already, she would have punched him at that point. But she was too intoxicated to do that yet.

They sat for a minute in silence before Ty finally started talking again.

"So, these two guys from my pool league, both weaker players but still having a blast, decide to start gambling, you know, just to work on their game, hone their skills. Not all gamblers are bad, some just want to improve. And he goes to the other guy, 'rack 'em fish.' Hehe. Well, the guy didn't know the first thing about how to rack the balls from what everyone could see. Hehe, funny stuff right?"

"Right?" Lucy laughed and agreed.

"So... while all this is happening, a few other players decide to check out what's going on, and it's league night so everything is supposed to be about league and fun, right? The Jukebox takes a break, and the room gets so quiet you could have heard a dime drop."

Lucy started to giggle a little, awkwardly.

"So he racks the balls up the best he can manage to, and the other player does a Happy Gilmore break, busting the balls up as hard as he can!"

Lucy looked in amazement at the story she was hearing. She seemed almost overwhelmed, but happy.

"The cue ball flies off the table and lands into the other player's crotch! Isn't that just fucking nuts?"

Lucy and Ty laughed together at this out loud. It was an amusing story, but Lucy wasn't laughing anymore. In fact, she stopped altogether and just listened. Something about the way Ty finished the story had woken Lucy up from her drunkenness.

Ty had clearly overstepped his boundary now by the way he was touching Lucy. And they both knew it.

"What? You mean kinda like this?"

Lucy swung her leg back and kicked Ty hard in the groin area. Ty yelled out loud. It must have hurt badly.

Lucy looked proud and said, "You can F yourself, Ty!"

Lucy got up and left the bar, while Ty looked at the bartender standing there laughing at the sight of him holding his man.

"I still think she really has a thing for me," Ty said to the male bartender.

The scary thing was, Ty wasn't even kidding. Ty had such an ego he might have just had her. Some women liked guys with that kind of confidence and swag. Lucy may or may not have been that kind of a woman.

Val and Jasper were now in downtown Saint Louis, home of the famous Arch. This was the Gateway to the West. The area was hopping and very much alive this evening. A few skyscrapers scraped against the dark skies as the two hustlers drove through the night in search of a game.

"There's a handicapped 9-ball tournament at a spot called Downtown Player's Bar and Grill near the Arch. I think we can get you in there at a low-game spot and you could win it."

Val was excited to be playing in a tournament for once. He grinned and looked over to Jasper in the vehicle.

"I'm hungry."

"Good. Stay that way. You'll shoot better hungry than on a full stomach, kid."

"Are we going to find action in here, too?"

"Maybe, maybe not. Let's just focus on snapping off this tournament first. While you do that, let me scout the place out. Listen, Val. You got to watch out for the house pro, Andy Quinn. Stay the hell away from him. If he asks you to play for money, just tell him no. You'd rather eat dirt than play him, cause if you play him, they will jack your handicap up if you win, not that you would, anyway..."

"Wait, I know him. I've seen him play. He is an incredible player."

"Yes. Like I said, we need to keep you under the radar and away from these knowns. For now, just take it slow. Follow my lead. Baby steps, kid."

They pulled up next to Downtown STL Player's Bar and Grill and parked.

Val and Jasper exited their car and entered the room. It was a lively place, even more so than Sharpshooter's. Players came strolling in behind them, and there was a player on every single table already. Some even had groups of players.

It was already 7 PM and the tournament was to begin in half an hour. Jasper forked over the entry fee of twenty dollars to the tournament director, Ernie. Ernie was the guy who ran this tournamen,t and he knew how to run them well. He had a lot of experience running tournaments, and that was why Jasper had trusted him. He was also exceptionally smart about banking balls. That was how he got the nickname Ernie Banks.

"Now, kid, if a guy named Ernie Banks asks you to play banks, you know what to tell him, right?"

"What?"

"What? What do you mean, 'what?' Are you a bank artist?"

"No, I guess not."

"Then don't play him banks. The guy is a bank champion. His nickname is Ernie Banks for a reason. Actually, he was called that for the first time when he tried to rob a bank twenty years ago. But still, he banks like a god."

Val took in Jasper's words. He finally got to an open table and played a few warm-up games, getting in stroke for the tournament. Five minutes later, the tournament had begun, on time as expected.

Ernie Banks announced the table assignments over the microphone.

They had Val ranked as a 5-level player, which was a bit too low for his speed. That was the advantage of being an unknown, though, and Jasper loved it. So did Val.

There were thirty-two players in the tournament, all strong locals except for a few knowns, Ernie Banks being one of them. Val's first match went by quickly. He beat his opponent five games to two.

Val stroked the balls in, and consequently 9-ball after 9-ball was potted. He felt strong getting all that weight, until he had to play another player with equal weight that shot pretty well. The guy was strong just like Val, and he ended up winning, knocking Val into the loser's bracket.

"Shit," Val was frustrated with himself.

He made it all the way to the final match from the loser's bracket. In a field of thirty-two players, he was in the finals when he had to face the house pro, Andy Quinn, who he would have to double dip to win. That meant beating him twice in a row, two sets. Andy was a pretty big guy, above-average sized. He was about a foot taller than Val. Andy was a very special kind of competitor who a lot of players feared and some had even lost their stroke for months after just playing a set with him.

Mr. Quinn was stroking some warm-up balls when Val came up to him.

"I guess it's me and you now, huh?"

Andy replied to Val's question by nodding his head and shooting a few practice shots.

Andy won the flip, and then said, "Rack 'em."

Val racked them up.

When Andy broke them, three balls went in quickly off the snap. He then only had six more to make in consecutive order. But since the layout wasn't simple, and there were few balls on the table, it was going to be a task getting the shape he wanted on these last balls before the 9-ball.

Andy was considered one of the best pool players in the area. That was part of why they had him going to such a high number in this tournament.

Andy had two balls tied up that needed to be either banked in or broken out at some point. It was the 5 and the 7-ball.

When he got to the five-seven tie-up he was forced to bank the 5-ball in. Andy did a few pump strokes, and then laid his cue on the table, lining up his shot path.

He got down on the ball so that the edge of his chin touched the cue stick.

Somehow, the ball didn't go in, and Andy had missed his bank.

It was then Val's turn to shoot. He had a relatively easy out from there as the balls were lined up perfectly for him. Val shot them in like he was taking out the trash. It was like picking apples for him.

Val made the out, sunk the 9-ball, and then got ready for the next break.

It was a five to twelve race, so the odds were probably in Val's favor.

Val ended up winning the first set.

There was 600 bucks for first, and 300 bucks for second place. Third place got the rest of the money. The bar had added money to the pot.

"Want to split?" Val asked Andy.

Andy agreed, only because of the weight he had to give up, and that was it. They had split first place and second place winnings together. They had each taken 450.

Jasper got up from his spectator chair and gave his apprentice a fist pump.

"Good job, kid. Hey, I'll be right back. I need to go outside and smoke. Not that I really need to, though."

The room wouldn't allow smoking inside but had a designated smoker's area just outside for addicts like Jasper. Jasper mingled with a few of the players outside while he puffed his cigarette. They cracked jokes as Jasper's voice carried throughout the smoker yard.

Back in the pool room, while Val was still licking his chops for winning that tournament, one of the locals was watching him. He was also observing him beat Quinn the first set, and that really got him going. Things like that didn't just go unnoticed in pool rooms.

That individual approached Val and started woofing at him in pure envy. Val looked over at him.

"Hey man, you must be a pro. You want to play some one hole?"

"One hole? Um … I have a backer. Give me a second."

Val looked around and didn't see Jasper anywhere. Jasper was nowhere in sight in the pool room currently.

"Umm.. like I said, I'm getting staked and…. I don't know where he went? Okay… yeah to be honest, I don't really play one hole. And I don't know you either, how you play…," Val said. And Val was just being himself at this point. He was no one-pocket player. He had heard of the game, observed it, but he had never actually competed in the game. Val was a 9-ball and 8-ball player strictly. One pocket sounded fun to him though.

"Oh, come on, Mister Pool Shark, you just beat the brains out of the best player, bar none, in the room… How could you refuse? What do ya mean you're not a one-hole player?"

Andy was still shooting balls, running racks for practice over on the bar table where he had played Val.

Val decided to play dumb like he had no idea.

"Oh really? And who was that?"

"Well, the pro of course. Andy Quinn. What haven't you heard of him? Yeah, he's the House Pro, and I just seen ya. You beat him five to seven to win the tournament."

"First of all, I had an insane amount of weight. And secondly, we split first and second place."

Who was this guy? Did Val even know him? Or his first name even? Val started to feel a little threatened by his aggression. So Val had to ask him.

"What's your name, anyway?"

"It's Chuck."

"Okay, look Chuck, I'm no professional. And if you think I am, you're dead wrong."

"Well, you walk like a pro, talk like a pro, you definitely hold a cue like a pro. I just saw you beat a pro. So maybe you just need to admit it: You're a pro! Now, let's play some one hole."

At this point Val had to tell him. He wasn't a sponsored player. Yeah, that was the kicker. He would simply tell him the truth. Chuck needed to know that Val was severely overrated. And he was still technically at amateur status. *Every dog has their day, right?*

"Okay, wise guy, I've got no sponsors, none. You don't see me playing on tv, do you? My name is Valentine. I'm a local player."

"Yeah, whatever you say... are we game or not?"

"Yeah, I'm game." Val said, mustering up the courage to venture into the unknown. One pocket was an unusual game to him and he wasn't sure how this one would end up. Val had very little experience in the ways of one hole.

They start out playing for fifty bucks a game. Chuck played a lot of strong defensive shots, then ran a few balls. He played a safety, ducked, then ran. Safety, duck and run. And he was brilliant at it. Val was off balance and felt a bit dizzy.

Val lost the first two games. He was in for 100 bucks now.

Val sat in his spectator chair when he suddenly recognized a voice from his left ear. He turned his head and it was his backer, Jasper.

"Kid, how much are you down?"

"100 bucks."

"Get out, now! Get out of the bet!" Jasper snapped at him, sounding ticked.

"No, I'll win it back. Stop treating me like a kid."

Jasper looked furious. He had never been so pissed off at someone he was trying to help make money.

"You're making all the wrong shots, kid. Just pay the man and quit!"

"I will. Just let me play this out. I'll get even, then we'll be done, okay?"

Val looked at the table as Chuck was running balls. He tried to ignore Jasper's pull.

"Look at me! Over here, Val! Look, you quit now, and you make money. You keep making these dumb shots, you will lose your ass."

Chuck sank the eighth ball, and it was Val's turn to break. He jumped out of his chair and racked the balls up, all fifteen.

Jasper peeled a 100-dollar bill from his wallet and threw it on the table in frustration.

"Here's your money, hot shot. We're done here!"

"Hey, Jasper!!"

"Quitting already?" Chuck asked. "I thought this guy was a champ."

Jasper proceeded and grabbed Val by the shirt collar.

"Sorry, mister, my son has a bit of a gambling problem. Son? What the hell are you doing pissing your life away gambling?"

Chuck giggled.

Jasper yanked him all the way outside to the smoking lounge.

Val asked him, "What the hell was that all about back there? That was my entertainment for the night!"

"Entertainment? No, you cannot play one pocket. I SAVED us money back there, that's what that was about!"

"Fine, I'll draw the line there. No more one pocket for money."

"Remember, this business is ninety percent how we respond to losing. If we are good losers, we win in the long run. It's alright now, just get over it, quit your cryin.'"

"I ain't crying." And Val wasn't crying at all. He was starting to admire Jasper and his ways, peculiar as they might seem.

"I think we're starting to make progress. I'm going to teach you some more shit tomorrow, alright, kid?"

Val and Jasper grabbed their cues and headed back to the county. On the way home, Jasper talked a great deal about the drills he planned to show Val, now that Val had his first tournament victory under his belt. He said that he would show Val how to make the cue ball land on any specific spot on the table, and on any kind of shot.

That same evening, Deon Williams ate at Red Lobster with Ashley. They drove separately, so Deon could have some alone time. They were just meeting up as friends, nothing too serious at this point.

While they ate, all he could think about was Jasper, or at least he was on his mind. The guy was a lowlife dummy, he thought to himself at dinner. Deon just wasn't the kind to intimidate a lowlife, but since Jasper had crossed the line he had to delegate it to a third party. And Deon had just the guy for the job.

Deon walked out of Red Lobster, said his goodbye to Ashley, and jumped into his Mustang. He drove for a while down the road. He then picked up his cell phone to make a call to his contact.

"Hey, hey, Vincent, how you doing, my man?"

"Good, good, Deon… what can I do for you?"

Vincent was the kind of guy who helped get people like Deon out of jams when they were owed a large amount of money. He was a debt collector.

"I need you to take care of somebody for me. He's in Saint Louis."

"What's this about, Deon? I'm a busy somebody. Can you tell me some more details?"

"Let's meet somewhere to talk. When can you be available?"

"Tomorrow morning. I can meet at Waffle House. Shoot me a time."

"10 AM. Sharp!"

Deon confirmed the time to meet and the address with Vincent.

9

The following morning it was raining cats and dogs outside, and Deon was in his Mustang scoping out the Waffle House, waiting for his contact to arrive. Deon didn't want any funny business. He was all about that bling bling this morning. He didn't care if he would have to throw Vincent a few bones for doing the dirty deed for him. The rain poured against Deon's vehicle and trickled down his windshield.

And without much delay, there was Deon's guy. He was a big guy in a hoody, stout, with a dark complexion. The man had thick skin.

Deon got out and met the man inside Waffle House. Vincent Donnie was sitting down already, and he didn't even take the time to get up to shake hands with or greet Deon.

Vincent stated firmly, "So…. What am I doing this for? You gotta give me some incentive."

"Half. Your stake is fifty percent for this job."

"Alright, I ain't wastin' my time… how much money you suspect this thug's got?

"Oh he's got money. Already did my homework. Should be under the bed. The guy is never home! Should be a pretty clean job. In and out…"

Vincent adjusted himself in his seat and ordered a coffee. Deon asked for a glass of milk for himself.

After a few minutes of silence the waitress came back with the drinks.

"Thanks, Miss," the gentlemen said in unison.

Deon continued, "Okay, the guy is about to get evicted from his apartment. He's a degenerate in his prime. Probably a bigger fool than I've ever come across. But… we NEED our cash."

"I'll do it for fifty percent. Just be patient. These kinds of hits take time. This one… might take a week or so from what I know. You got the address?"

"Yes."

Deon reached into his jacket and pulled out a piece of paper. He then slid the paper across the table for Vincent.

The following day, Jasper and Val were exchanging words about billiards at the house. They were discussing how things were going. Jasper had asked Val how he felt about everything, and Val seemed relatively comfortable, but at the same time wanted to understand more about Jasper and why those guys were after him. Why hadn't he just paid them when he had the chance? Or even paid them in the first place, the first time?

"Look, Jasper, I really appreciate what you are doing for me, but I just want to know…"

Jasper interrupted him, "As long as we are making money, and kid, we are making it… you know it, and I know it."

Jasper puffed a cigarette creating a circular cloud of smoke in front of his lips while sifting through the cash winnings. He looked through 100 dollar bill after 100 dollar bill, inspecting each one individually like they all had a different personality.

Jasper spoke again, "Money, kid, it's a thing of beauty ain't it? Winning money…"

Val was getting hungrier for the cash. And so was Jasper. Deep inside, Val wanted to be Jasper's best friend. He was hooked on being Jasper's friend, his buddy, his apprentice.

"I need a nickname, Jasp," Val said.

"No, that's where you're wrong. You need everything but a nickname."

"Fast Valentine, Speedy Valentine? Something cool like that. I don't know…"

"You're right, you don't know. We've made a little over 3K together. Now, here's your take, kid."

Jasper handed Val some cash. Val counted it quickly. It didn't add up to the appropriate figure or the amount he had hoped for.

"So… this is 1K… I thought you said we made a total of 3K?"

"Yes… and??"

"Shouldn't I get 1500?"

Jasper laughed and said, "Your cut is a third."

Val was a little confused by this and possibly frustrated.

"I made all the shots… I won the games."

"I put you in, numb nuts. Without me putting you in and staking you, you wouldn't have stood a chance to win anything. Don't you get it?"

Jasper stood up from the couch and continued his rant, "A thirty percent cut is great. I'm a good backer. Plus, there's a lot more cash to be made in this town. We're not finished yet."

Marty and Lucy were discussing things over the phone. Since Val had pretty much gone rogue and abandoned Lucy, it was Lucy's mission to either get him back to ground zero or dump him. Marty would know what to do.

"I just think he should be more realistic about his life. That's all," Lucy commented.

"I agree, I agree…," Marty replied. "Okay, I've got an idea."

"What?" Lucy asked quickly and curiously.

"Okay, I know this is going to sound dumb, but I think we need to call Mommy out on this one."

"Marty, you've got to be…," Lucy laughed.

"I'm serious. I think she might have an idea. Something we can do to help him get a job. Get something going for him."

"She lives not too far away, actually. I think we could go to her house and tell her what's going on at least."

And that settled it. They were going to Val's mom to get some advice and much needed help.

The leaves were turning orange and brown, falling from the trees now. A fall atmosphere was setting in. Their course had altered slightly. They were in a small bar with one old eight-foot pool table. Jasper instructed Val to close his eyes as he got down on whitey.

"Wait, what?"

Jasper insisted that Val do it and just close his eyes. He didn't even explain why yet. He just said it.

"Close your eyes and stroke the ball as if you see it in your mind."

Now he was starting to understand. It was a drill, of course.

Val went ahead and closed his eyes after getting down on his shot. He did a few pump strokes and then hit it. The cue ball collided with the object ball and the object ball rattled against the rail. MISS!

Val missed his first attempt so Jasper grabbed a hold of the cue ball and placed it back in proximity to Val.

Val closed his eyes again and stroked the ball. Miss, again.

"If you can learn to shoot with your eyes shut, you can master muscle movement memory. Do you know what muscle movement memory is?"

Jasper continued while Val still had his eyes closed.

"You can open your eyes now, kid."

He opened his eyes and shook his head at the question.

"Muscle movement memory is exactly what it sounds like. It just means keeping your cue stick steady. Now, try this."

Jasper took out a scarf and put it around Val's head so that he was blindfolded.

"If you can shoot pool blind, you can win championships. We're not going anywhere tonight until you can make at least ten in a row."

They were at a hole-in-the-wall bar. They were some of the only people there, too. Nobody was going to bother them or woof at them at this place, Val thought. This concept made him feel right at home.

Jasper had instructed Val to shoot blindfolded and make ten balls in a row, long, straight-in-corner-pocket shots.

"I want you to learn to freewheel. Freewheeling will help you to make every ball you shoot at with little to no thought and piss your opponent off in the process."

Val laughed and took off the blindfold, frustrated with himself and a little uneasy, too.

"You've gotta be kidding me! Who am I, the karate kid? This has got to be a joke!"

"Um, no it ain't. Yeah, you better get used to wearing that cause we are not leaving till ya master this drill."

"Whatever you say, old timer, but anyway what does free-wheeling even mean in the first place?"

"Freewheeling is the art of playing pool without worrying about anything, having no fear of missing, and shooting with your eyes closed is the perfect drill to train you to do just that. You're going to be one sick, freewheelin' S.O.B. after I'm done with you."

Val was not used to being instructed like this. Jasper had sort of changed the momentum, the direction of their mission. Val didn't see this as a very good use of their time at first, but after a few more attempts, he started to make balls in without even looking at the cue ball. The best he could do was three or four in a row. But what Jasper had demanded of him was an insurmountable task, it seemed.

Val continued to stroke the balls, making some here and there, but missing some as well. Freewheeling was actually a slang billiard term and you didn't hear the term too often in the community anymore. It was a rare instance that someone had actually used that word in a small local bar like the one Jasper and Val were frequenting that day.

Jasper grabbed a drink of Bud Light and hung out at the bar for a minute. He was making small talk with a young lady there. Jasper was just being Jasper, while Val continued his training.

"Keep stroking it. And hang on to that blind fold until you can do at least eight out of ten."

Jasper knew the sport of billiards well. He knew that if he could train this kid to be a leader in the billiards community and make money off of him, he could eventually get his life back and clear his debt, not to mention his conscience. That is, if such a person had a conscience. Val knew it wasn't right what the old timer did with those players back then. But the question was, did he know it was wrong? Did Jasper want to pay them what he owed them, or was he simply too much of a degenerate? It was a question of ethical standards, right versus wrong.

10

Vincent Donnie had pulled up right next to Jasper's apartment in his vehicle. Vincent drove a white-colored Hyundai Sonata, a pretty sporty looking car if you asked anybody on the block. Vincent had the tinted windows too, which added to the flare. Vince checked the address he had and made sure it was the right place. It was. He pulled out his phone and took a snapshot of the street, the house, and all surroundings. He covered all angles and made sure he knew the location well before he was to enter.

Vince turned off his camera on his iPhone and got out of the vehicle. He quickly walked up to the front door and started knocking very loudly. If Jasper wasn't home, it would make things easier. He had been told the money was not very well hidden, but possibly underneath the bed. That was the skinny, but sometimes they were wrong. He knocked again, harder this time. No one came to the door.

Vince was getting impatient so he decided to rush things a little and instead of homeward bound he was headed through the door with a credit card. He took out his wallet and pulled out the Visa. He then slipped it through the lock in the door, doing it the old-fashioned way. This lock was an easy one to break, but wait. What about the neighbors? Did he look suspicious? He suddenly realized he had taken this scenario for granted. A man of his stature and ability shouldn't have to bust open a door in broad daylight.

"Fuck this..." he cursed to himself.

Realizing quickly his error, he stepped back away from the front porch and fled the scene. He retired to his vehicle and looked at his phone again. Back to his usual self, he analyzed the photos he had taken earlier, and the pictures spoke volumes to him. They told him a story that he liked very much.

Val, in the middle of his drill, received a phone call. It was Marty. Marty said hello, and advised Val that he needed to have a word with him in person. Val hung up the phone. About a minute later he received a text. Again, it was Marty. The message read, "Your Mom Esther is ill. You should go see her asap bro!"

Val's heart skipped a beat as he stroked the ball in. He took off the blindfold and looked over at Jasper. He yelled, "Ten out of ten!"

Jasper looked over from the bar as he was sitting down having a round of beers. He smiled, got up from his chair, and walked over to Val. Jasper said, "Let's go."

While they drove along, Jasper and Val talked about billiards and what their next spot would be. Val received another text from Marty. This time it said, "And if you want Lucy back you better hurry. Ty was hitting on her the other night."

Val started typing a message and then deleted it. He was getting stressed. What was a guy to do?

"Hey, let's call it a night. What do you say?"

Jasper took him home at that point. They both agreed it was a good opportunity for a break. Val had just shot the best drill of his life and made ten balls in a row blindfolded.

The following morning Val made a phone call to his mother to let her know that he was coming over to visit. Their conversation was short because Esther didn't live that far away and Val was already on his way to see her.

At the front door, Val knocked and was shortly after greeted by his mom.

"Hey son, come on in. Wow, you look like death!"

Val and Esther hugged at the door. Val walked inside, and they both sat down in the living room.

"Yeah, I lost my job."

"What??"

"Yes, I know it's been rough, but I met this guy who took me out, and we've been making money together."

"Doing what???"

Esther looked curious. How was Val going to respond to that question? It was one of those moments when you knew the question was coming but weren't prepared to answer it yet.

"Just playing pool, action games," Val replied, sounding dumb and knowing it, too.

"What happened at the car place where you worked?"

"Well, they fired me. DM Steve fired me. He said I wasn't being effective with the customers, taking care of customers and slacking with customer service, all that jazz."

"So what is going on with your head? Are those pool players taking advantage of you?"

"No, not at all. They aren't. It's just there are these two players. One thinks he is the talk of the town, hitting on my girlfriend and stuff. He asked me to join this league. And the other is making me money on the side. He's like my pool mentor."

"Mentor? What? Have you been gamblin' and losing your shirt?"

Val inhaled and thought to himself, taking his time to make sure this conversation was played out appropriately and honestly.

"No. Okay, I'm going to be honest with you Mom, I love you and want you to be happy. But I am not being taken or losing money that I don't have. This guy, Jasper, is helping me get by while I look for a new job."

"Hon, it's great you're doing something that you love, and I like the fact that you are keeping an open mind about it, still looking for other opportunities. But, son, hustling pool is dangerous. You can't expect to make a living doing that. This guy you met, he's the hustler type, isn't he?"

"Hustler or not, he's helping me live my dreams."

"Well, if you are making money, you're making money. I just want you to have something that lasts."

There was a pause in the conversation. Esther got up and made Val a glass of water. She handed it to him. Val took a big gulp from the glass and thanked his mother.

"Hey what do you say we go out tonight together as family? I know a place down the road you might like. It's called One Eyed Fred's. You know, have a drink, some bonding time?"

"Yes, that sounds like a good idea," Val replied as his frown turned into a smile.

"Okay, I'll drive!"

Now, one Eyed Fred's wasn't nearly as nice a place as it used to be because apparently Esther thought it was the real deal of the pool scene back in the day, and it might just have been.

In a game of 8-ball, Val's mother broke the balls up. The balls clashed together forming a Dolly Parton break.
"I can't believe you have never been here! This place used to be my hangout place as a kid."

"I didn't think you went out to places like this as a kid. Haha."

Val got down on the ball and swished a ball in. And then another and another, getting a bit out of line eventually. He then intentionally missed a shot to let his mother shoot.

His mother surprised him and ran the entire rack from that point.

"Ha, I guess this game runs in the family, huh? You're not the only one in this family who knows how to hold a cue." Esther pretended to blow off some smoke from the tip of her cue and giggled. Val smiled back at her.

Val won the next game they played.

"Okay, last game."

"Rack 'em up, Mom!"

Val's mother bent over the table to rack the balls up, while Val checked the rack and then explained to her how they must all be frozen tight.

"Mom, the balls have to all be frozen together like this." Val took the rack and moved it back and forth over the spot until there were no gaps in the rack of balls.

Val noticed his mother's hands were shaking when she was racking the balls. He could see Esther when she was attempting to rack. Her hands shook violently.

"Mom, are you alright? Your hands… You're trembling!"

"I'm fine. No, keep playing."

Val broke the balls and they went boom! The balls spread apart everywhere and a ball nearly flew off the table, but landed just inside the cloth, making it a legal break.

"So this is your life, huh, son?"

"I am working my way up. Ya know, pool is tough. It is harder than playing golf, some say."

"Sure! Is there money in it?"

"At a certain level there is, yes."

After that game they drove home, and Esther was pretty quiet most of the ride until she opened her mouth finally.

"Son, I do have a sickness, actually. You saw me shaking back there, right? Well tremors are a side effect. I was diagnosed with brain cancer. It is curable. But I just don't have enough money to afford the brain surgery. Medical costs are high, and insurance only pays for a portion of it!"

Val's stomach dropped and his face turned white as a ghost. What did he just hear? Was this a nightmare?

Val frowned and replied, "Oh my God, Mom. You're kidding right? That's the worst thing I've ever heard! How much money do you need, Mom?"

Val suddenly became teary-eyed.

"About 15,000 dollars, son. But don't worry about me. I gotta kick the bucket someday, don't I?"

"No, don't you ever say something like that. I'm going to help you! I'm going to get you treatment. There's got to be a way."

"Don't worry about me, son. Just do what you love. That will be enough to make me happy!"

Esther smiled at him, her beloved son.

Esther and Val hugged one last time before Val left. Val had problems of his own and now this? His mother had brain cancer! What would Val do now? His mother wanted him to keep living his dreams.

But could he make sufficient money to pay for medical treatment doing what he was doing now? Probably not.

"You be careful out there, son. This ain't the wild west, ya hear?"

"Yes, mother."

"I love you, son."

"Mom, I love you too. And I promise, I'm going to help you out with those medical costs!"

Val returned to his car and drove home. That night he settled into bed with Lucy and said a prayer for his mother and that he would find the money she needed, somehow, someway. Was there hope for them?

11

It was in Val's hay day running around with Jasper that he had taken a drastic turn in life, and he would never be or feel the same again. Pool was taking over a big part of his time and energy. Jasper was gaining control over him.

The amount they were making was one thing, and those medical costs were another. Val had to come up with a way to make the bank. He had the State Tour coming up soon for Missouri, which paid out a lot of cash for the winners. There were also a few other options for him. Val knew that if he could do well in a big pool tournament it would be a very nice bonus that he could put towards Esther. He wanted to make Esther happy and get her the treatment she so needed.

Val rode in the car with Jasper on the way to a pool room the following evening. They were headed to a place in Tennessee called The Pool Room Bar and Grill. It was one of the bigger pool rooms in the area they were headed to, and there would be action. Traffic was light that night.

"So, Jasper, how much money we talking here? How does that tournament pay out for the winners?"

"Which one, kid? You are talking about the State Tour?"

"Yeah, that's right... that one."

"Well, it pays more money every year depending on the number of players. Last year they had sixty-four top shooters from Missouri, both pros and semi-pros. This year could be a big one. But they usually pay around 20K for first."

Val had butterflies in his stomach. That would be enough to get his mother out of the jam she was in financially and pay for that treatment, he thought to himself. Val's mother needed at least 15,000 dollars to afford her brain surgery, which would cure her for at least five years. And time was ticking.

"So, why did you have me wear this ugly shirt? I'm embarrassed to be wearing it in a pool room. Is this going to be some kind of trick?"

"Haha, well kid, that goofy yellow, collared shirt is no trick, but it is going to be part of the act you're about to play. I need you to act dumber than a two-dollar bill so that this will work."

The two road players sat next to each other at a dinner table in The Pool Room in the city of Nashville, TN. They had finally gotten out of Missouri for a while. They were going to try to settle down with their home state and take over some other territory.

Clouds of smoke filled the room in various packets, one here and one there. The room was smoking allowed, of course, so Val would have to adjust his eyes to the distraction. When smoke gets in your eyes it makes it a little bit harder to see the outline of the balls and sometimes even affects your ability to think strategically about the game.

Jasper spoke to Val.

"Alright, kid. You're going to sit on the sidelines this time. But if I signal you, call you up to the table, you're going to play with me, alright?"

"Is this another hustle?"

Val looked a little upset, but inside he was burning with excitement and passion for the game. Jasper dodged the question.

"Just sit here and pretend you're my son. We're going to steamroll these guys."

"Just tell me what you're going to do… I'm curious… C'mon, man…"

"Back in the old days, I knew this guy. This player, he inspired me. The way he cut the ball down the long rail was so incredible it put everyone watching in a hypnotic trance. The guy literally ran more racks than he racked in his lifetime, and I mean he had a very hard time missing. But when he did, it was like the earth stood still, ya hear? So, one time I seen 'em hustle these guys with his sister shooting with both hands, left and right-handed."

Val looked very intrigued by all this. He almost had the goose-bumps forming on his arms to where his hair follicles were nearly standing straight up. Val was definitely interested in this character.

"What was his name? Did he have a nickname?"

"It was Louie. Everyone called him Saint Louie Louie, because he was from Saint Louis."

"Is he still around?"

"No, kid."

"Why not?"

"He's no longer with us, kid. I'm, I'm sorry. But all you need to know is what I told you. And that he was probably the most charismatic player in any room he was in."

As Jasper lit his cigarette, the Eagles hit song "Back in the Fast Lane" played on the Jukebox.

Whoever Louie was, Jasper sure thought highly of him. Apparently from what Val later learned from Jasper, Louie Roberts could outrun the Ghost in 9-ball shooting with both hands, switching back and forth with his right hand and then left hand, which Val personally found simply incredible. Val quickly saw where this hustle was headed.

Playing the Ghost in 9-ball is a game that a lot of pros practice to get in stroke that involves playing against an imaginary opponent. If you miss a ball, you lose the game. The catch is you get ball in hand after the break if you don't scratch. And if you run out to the 9-ball, you win.

Jasper put out his cigarette, squishing it into the ashtray, and got up from his seat. He walked over to a couple drunks playing pool on a nearby table. Jasper had a beer in his hand and took a long gulp of it.

"So… what you potheads want to do? I'm drunker than a dead skunk…"

"This guy is off the air," the one player said to his friend, whispering quietly.

"Yeah, he's a nut job alright."

"I'm not any good at pool, but my buddy here, Sam, might play you. Sam?" The guy kicked Sam in the leg and winked at him as if he knew it would be a good game.

Jasper turned around and looked at Val giving him a subtle nod. Then he looked back at the two boys.

"I'm looking for a game. Yay or nay?" Jasper asked.

The two boys both looked at him for a while like he was a loony. Sam just remained quiet for a few seconds.

"What's that I hear? Crickets?" Jasper pressed on.

"I'll play ya, let's get our gamble on!" Sam finally said.

"How about a little 9-ball?"

So they agreed to play 9-ball, ten bucks a game, to keep it friendly for now.

Jasper lost every game, four games straight at The Pool Room. The two guys snickered as Jasper missed every ball he shot at, but what they probably didn't realize was he was playing with his wrong hand. His good hand was his left hand and he was playing with his right for the money games.

Jasper was down only forty dollars when he decided to change it up a bit.

"Forty... here's what I owe you. Alright, okay, how about this, Sam? Bet! Bet everything you've got and the car keys. Point to anybody over there at the bar to play with me and I'll partner 'em... we will play you doubles with your buddy."

Jasper pointed to Sam's friend and continued his woofing, "We'll play against you scotch doubles, and I'll even switch shooting hands, and shoot left-handed instead this time. What do you say Sam? A hundred bones a rack?"

"Sounds an awful lot like a hustle, mister, but I'll give it a whirl. Dave, let's do this."

Sam consulted with Dave and walked over and found him a partner. But there was a problem. He walked right past Val who was sitting down observing, and picked an old man over at the bar sitting down drinking.

"I can't play with no drunk. I'm ALREADY drunk, you fool. Bet's off. Unless ya pick someone at least sober and young," Jasper tried to explain, as he felt about as dumb as any drunk in the bar.

At this point if he hadn't picked Val there were going to be problems, because Val was the guy, the ace in the hole for this money game. Jasper needed him to beat these guys.

Sam and Dave talked it over after what Jasper had said. Before making any more moves, they thought about this scenario.

Before the two picked another partner, Val had done some thinking of his own. His nerdy outfit had not sold them apparently. He knew the game plan was already jacked up, so he decided to act on instinct and spoke up for himself as Dave and Sam walked past him a second time.

"Hey, you looking for a doubles partner?" Val asked, looking dumb.

"Yes, and what's it to you, kid?"

"I'll play."

They agreed that Val fit the part. Val ended up getting picked finally for the big money game.

"Alright, kid we are betting 100 dollars a game with these fools," Jasper said.

"Put your big boy pants on. Miss a few shots here and there. It won't be even close," Jasper whispered to Val.

The first game went completely in their favor and they were up 100 dollars quicker than they wanted to be.

The second game, Val missed what was a very difficult shot, making it look tough as he should have. It was then their turn to shoot. They ran the rest of the rack and got down to the 8-ball. It was a tough shot on the eight though, a cut shot all the way up the rail.

The 8-ball jarred in the corner pocket. MISS!

It was Jasper and Val's turn to shoot, and they had an easy out from there. Wide open table for them. Jasper and Val made quick work of the balls. Game number two was over. They won that game too.

Pretty soon they were up 500 bucks. And at that point, their opponents had thrown in the towel.

"Well, well, here's your money. Five hundred bucks. We're done," Dave said looking over at Sam, who agreed.

"You shoot pretty straight for a lefty, lemme guess, you're a righty, too?"

They had caught on that they had been played. Sam and Dave both knew it, too. Sam looked at Dave. Dave looked at Sam.

Sam took a right-handed swing at Jasper's face. Jasper swiftly ducked and dodged the hook. At the same time, he pushed Sam out of the way, shoving him all the way to the bar. He then turned around and grabbed hold of Val. They grabbed their cues and ran out of the door.

"What you trying to do? Get us into a bar fight? Damn!"

"Get in the car, kid!"

Val hopped in as the two angry men followed in hot pursuit. Jasper turned the keys in the ignition and the engine made a couple grunts before starting. It started. The two players they had just hustled, Dave and Sam, had run after them out the door. They looked around for them, in every direction. They saw them.

"Let's get outta here!" Jasper said and backed up out of his parking spot next to the pool room's entrance.

On the road, Jasper had some words for his young apprentice about what had happened that night. Val wasn't sure he wanted to go along with all that. It was hard for him to stomach, sort of.

"You almost got us both killed back there, man!" Val exclaimed.

"Look kid, we are building a future for you. The more of these little bets we can get into, the more tournaments I can put you in," he explained. "See, all these hustles and side games are going to give you skin thick enough to intimidate even some of the nation's top pros."

You weren't going to make it very far in pool without making enemies first. Like they say, if you don't have enemies then you don't stand for anything. Jasper wanted Val to stand up for something, like they were doing. And Val was also standing up for himself.

12

Val and Jasper talked and decided not to drive so far anymore, realizing that they probably hadn't done enough in this area quite yet to look for action elsewhere. It wasn't a bad idea going to Tennessee, but at the same time they still needed to claim their own territory and make a stance on their home turf.

So the two of them went to downtown Saint Louis again to check out a new place that had just opened up in the area called The Shooter's Downtown Club. The place was hopping with players in action. Money was being exchanged on the fly here, and there was only one table left open. Jasper and Val quickly got on it.

They started hitting balls together, practicing and warming up loosely, nothing too serious yet. And then Jasper received a phone call from an anonymous number. He picked up his phone and pressed the accept call option on his Android.

"Hello?"

Jasper heard some funny noises in the background, but nothing coherent or easy to understand.

"Hello?" Jasper said again.

Still he heard nothing but awkward background noise.

"Is this Jasper?" A low-pitched voice asked.

"Speaking…" Jasper replied. He temporarily excused himself from playing with Val and stepped outside.

"I need you to listen to me. Come to 23rd Street in Downtown by the Arch so we can collect our debt. It's a neutral location. I'm waiting for you there."

"Wait a minute, who the hell is this? And who do I owe money to? I hope this isn't…"

"I'm a debt collector. I have been asked to collect for Deon Williams. He is not the kind of man you want to disappoint.

Please cooperate or there will be repercussions," the voice said solemnly.

Jasper hung up the phone. He didn't want to stand for this intimidation at all. He didn't like the way it was going down. If he was going to pay those guys, at least he should have a chance to win it back first. Jasper didn't feel like they were being very decent and civil about this. *How long ago did that happen, anyway?*

Jasper ran back into the pool room.

"Who called?"

"Don't worry about it, kid," Jasper said avoiding the question completely. "Look, I've been meaning to tell you, I think your game has taken on a new level, a new form since you started to learn how to freewheel, and... and I just wanted to tell you how much that means to me, kid. You, you're like a son to me. Okay? I'm proud of you."

Val looked at Jasper and almost wanted to cry, thinking of who Jasper was, and his real father who he had never met. *Who was Jasper?*

Val remained silent in his thoughts.

"See what's going on over there? It's a ring game," Jasper leaned his head towards a group of young guys shooting pool, having fun on a nine-foot table. They were playing some kind of group game for money. Jasper had called it a ring game.

"This is your chance to really do something here, kid."

"What's a ring game?"

"It's 9-ball, only with three or more players on the same table, playing the same game."

"Okay, cool. I'm going to go see if I can jump in," Val said and rushed forward to get in the game. But before he could go too far, Jasper grabbed him by the shoulder and pulled him back.

"Listen to me, before you go over there I want ya to develop a kind of style for yourself, you know, get into a rhythm here. You ever seen that Justin Bergman play 9-ball? Very strong rhythm player and ring player. Just hop in there and try to shoot like him."

"Shouldn't I just focus on my own game, though? Isn't that what everyone else does?"

"Yeah, but listen, everyone has to start somewhere, and you're new to this game. Ring is different. All those players you see on tv started out by being a student of the game. So… be a student!"

"Okay, I'll do my best."

"Have fun and learn something while I scope out the room," Jasper said and let him go.

Val hurried on to the scene and stopped, observing them run out and finish the last rack before asking if he could get in.

The other players agreed. The more the merrier. Val was in now.

When it got to be his turn to shoot, one of the players looked over at him and informed him that it was his shot. They were playing five bucks on the 5-ball and five on the 9-ball per player.

Val got down on the 4-ball after the last player missed. He made the ball straight in from one end of the table to the other, staying down on his shot until the ball dropped in the pocket. Then he stood up straight and did a subtle strafe to the left, lining up his next shot. He got down on the 5-ball and speared it in, a tough angle shot that he made look easy.

The cue ball rolled down the length of the table and just when it passed the spot where he needed it to lay rest, Val uttered, "Easy greasy!"

Val now had what was a tougher shot than he had naturally wanted on this ball. He focused and took his time doing a few pump strokes while contemplating the path.

Val made the next shot with grace and anticipated where the cue ball was going by sort of following it off the rail and around the table with his eyes and movements.

One of the players shouted at him, "Who is this guy?"

"Name is Val, Val Madonna."

Val had never felt so cool in his entire life playing pool, or in fact had he ever felt that cool in his entire life outside of pool. Ring games were the bees knees of action games, he thought to himself as he speared in the last moneyball, the 9-ball.

The other players threw down ten dollars each, and Val collected the cash.

Val's next break demonstrated perfect fundamentals and posture. It was a monster break.

"Kid's got a monster break doesn't he?" Jasper said to a gentleman that he was drinking with at the bar.

Jasper received another phone call from the unknown collector. He ignored it this time, immediately pressing the end call button on his cell phone.

Val ran this rack out quicker than the last one and collected the money again.

"I'm out, guys," one of the other players exclaimed.

"Me too, this guy's just too good. Who let 'em in?"

Val took his winnings and walked over to Jasper at the bar. Jasper was drinking a shot of Rum and Coke.

"Make any new friends, kid?"

"Not exactly Jasper, hehe."

"Ha, I figured."

A few of the players that Val was playing with a minute ago were whispering to each other, talking about Val behind his back.

"The guy is no slouch. He's a ringer! What was I supposed to do?" the kid explained to his buddy.

"Fucking highway robbery, man!"

13

The time flew by like an airplane through a runway and it was already past midnight. Jasper and Val just decided to hang out and relax at a nearby casino. They walked in like a couple of cocky, Hollywood hotshots. They really were quite the pair, the two of them, like two peas in a pod.

The casino they had entered was called the Lumiere. The bright lights reminded Jasper of Vegas, and as they walked inside they could hear Bobby Darin's "Dream Lover" playing, one of Jasper's favorite artists. It had all roped Val in, as he quickly found a blackjack table and sat down next to a couple other folks. Jasper had taken this as an opportunity to teach Val a life lesson. So, instead of stopping him, Jasper restrained himself and stepped back, observing. He knew Val didn't have more than a hundred bucks on him, as that was as much as he would have let him have in his possession. A good stake horse knows how to keep his money from the people he backs at times. This was the time to let Val do most of the work and then, when it was over, let the words come out. After an hour or so of looking at his watch and checking out the women at the casino bar, Jasper got restless enough to go over to the blackjack table where Val was playing. Val had, coincidentally, just lost his last five dollars. He sat up and cursed.

"You ready to leave now?" Jasper asked.

"Yeah!" Val almost yelled.

In the car, Jasper spoke about the casino like he had been there many times before.

"Ya know Val, I just want you to learn before you get too old that you can make more money playing pool than at the boat."

"Just something to do, right?"

"I'm going to use another analogy that might help you under-stand even better. Gambling at the casino is like climbing a steep mountain of sand dunes. With every step forward you take two steps backwards. The power of the sand is very difficult to combat. You ever tried climbing up something like this on all fours? I tell ya what, kid, it ain't no picnic. Believe me!"

"Can't people just quit when they are ahead?" Val asked.

"Just imagine yourself at the very bottom of a sand dune. The way down is very smooth and it doesn't take much effort to get to the bottom. When you reach the abyss, you gaze into the waters in front of you, and it is a magnificent sight. But, what you don't see, what you don't realize, is that it's going to be a hell of a way back up to the top. Every time you win money at the casino, it is like you are taking a step forward in the sand dune. But really, you're taking two steps backwards. It's a cycle of pain that makes the climb highly dangerous and difficult. For those people who can't endure the climb, there is a rescue team. The punchline is you're a solid pool player, way better than a gambling fool, or crapshooter, so don't get the two confused. You can do things on the pool table that most of those cardsharps back there never would have even thought of. But you can't win against the house! Remember that, alright kid?" Jasper said, and concluded the pitch that he had contrived for his pool-shooting apprentice while skillfully lighting a cigarette, with one hand on the steering wheel and one holding the butt.

"Is that right?" Val replied with a chuckle.

Val was inspired to say the least. His drive suddenly turned to pool. All his focus and energy was suddenly turned away from pure betting. Val could then put all his energy into a game of ninety-five percent skill, only five percent luck: Pocket Billiards.

Jasper went on to explain how the rescue team to the gambler is like the Gambler's Anonymous meeting or the 1-800-BET-S-OFF phone line.

"Is there really a place like this somewhere?" Val inquired.

"Yes, there are several places like that in Michigan, called the Sleeping Bear Dunes. Anyway, the house always wins. Every casino is like that. My advice to you is quit while you can."

Val really appreciated Jasper's efforts in this regard. He was clearly the wise one when it came to money and betting. Val left without losing more than fifty bucks, but learned a lesson he would never forget. The damage was very minimal, and at that Val had learned a great lesson. Val had also realized something important about billiards. In pool, you are so driven to make money and win that it may have just simply rubbed off on him in that casino. His motivations and efforts in pool had translated to the casino when they had first walked in and seen the lights. In pool you sort of have to create your own luck, and tip the odds in your favor. This is like in blackjack. The hidden, underlying conflict is that in blackjack, you cannot do much else to create luck other than play the cards that are laid on the table, playing basic strategy. This will never be comparable to the amount of finesse and dexterity that is a requirement in 9-ball or any pool game. Val had just confessed to this and made a vow to not ever go back there. Val knew he simply could not control the outcome at the boat nearly as much as he could in the pool world.

They pulled in to a parking lot at a seedy bar in downtown Saint Louis. A throaty, older man came up to Val inside the dive bar. Next to him sat an excitable looking character in a wheelchair, also an older gentleman around the same age as his friend.

"Hey, my name is Michael, and this is my buddy, Eric. You guys want to play some scotch doubles 8-ball with us?" The man asked, standing right next to Jasper and Val.

Jasper stepped over Val and interrupted before he could utter even a word.

"Val and I would be delighted. Let's play for something though…"

"Okay, okay, let's keep this friendly. How about the loser pays for a round of beers for all of us?"

Val said that sounded fine, and Jasper agreed.

Eric, the guy in the wheelchair, broke the balls and the games started. Val and Jasper won the first few games while Eric and Michael continually, game after game, bought them more drinks.

It was Eric's turn to shoot, and he had a tough angle on the cue ball so he equipped his extension tool for reaching the ball.

"Hey, wait a minute, Eric, you have to have one foot on the floor, don't you?" Val asked.

Eric blushed and hesitated.

Val and Jasper started cracking up at the comment. Their opponents chuckled a little.

"Haha damn, that was mean, kid."

Eric then continued, "I don't think so… I'm going to run out!"

"You sure you're going to do that? Haha…" Jasper added.

"No, but what I am going to do is make these balls disappear while you two suckers serve us drinks," he retorted.

The round dinner table next to the pool table was stacked, completely covered with empty beer bottles from their drinking games. All four of them felt utterly filthy as they became more and more intoxicated.

"Oh my gosh Jasp, I can't drink anymore," Val said.

Val felt his stomach getting sick so he rushed to the trash can. Nothing. He rushed on back to the pool table.

"I feel sick."

He felt even queasier this time so he hurried on back to the trash can near the entrance. He leaned over it and tried desperately to let it out. Jasper over at the table spoke to the two players.

"I think my friend has had enough drinks. Hehe, let's call it a night."

Michael and Eric both nodded and agreed.

On the way back home, Jasper and Val spoke about pool, and pool tournaments, and of course the State Tour coming up in a few months.

"Are you going to be okay to drive, Jasp man?" Val asked him. The car was swerving a little. They were driving home on the highway. There was not any traffic in sight.

"We should have called a cab," Val added, knowing full well that Jasper was intoxicated. The funny thing was, so was Val.

"What, you want to drive?" Jasper inquired.

Suddenly, they saw a bright set of lights ahead of them. Val noticed it right away and identified them as a semi-truck.

Jasper was veering into the left lane slowly as the truck approached. Val grabbed the steering wheel from the passenger seat and jerked the wheel to the right. They only just avoided colliding into the semi-truck.

"Shit!! Alright, get out! I'm driving from here. You almost got us into a collision, you old goof."

Jasper stopped the car and pulled to the side of the road.

Val got in the driver's seat and stepped on the gas pedal, a little tipsy still as well. Val was driving too fast on the freeway when from behind they saw a pair of headlights go on out of nowhere from the side of the road.

That vehicle started following them from behind.

After about a minute went by, the pursuing vehicle made themselves known to them and three bright flashing lights went off on the hood: red, white, and blue. They were in big trouble now.

Luckily they were only going about ten over. Val stopped the car immediately and pulled over to the curbside. He tried to remain calm and lax, but it was nearly impossible. Val couldn't afford a ticket!

The cop pulled right behind them and got out of his car. Val rolled down the window as the cop spoke first.

"Do you realize how fast you were going there, son?"

"Yeah, I was fifteen over. I'm sorry officer, but..." Val begged. The officer was hard-nosed on speeding violations, and Val and Jasper knew they were both doomed.

Jasper leaned over to speak and to add some degree of levity, "Better check the back…. He's got some pool paraphernalia."

Everyone at the scene laughed out loud at this, including Jasper and then Val chimed in and said, "I was driving my drunk friend home from pool league. He needed a lift."

The officer handed them a ticket and continued.

"Well, I hope you boys won, cause I'm writing you all a ticket! Have a good night and be safe." Jasper knew he had embarrassed Val, so he agreed to cover the ticket expense. This made Val feel a whole lot better.

14

It had been weeks since Val and Lucy had talked to each other. Actually, they had both gone completely rogue for a while due to the money and job situation. It was a two-way street. Of course, they still lived together. The problem was not Lucy, or Val, or money, though. The problem was inherent in their paths and what they both wanted to do with their lives. What Val wanted or should do with his life was largely influenced by how good he was getting at pool and Jasper. Marty wanted Val to get his head out of his rear and start applying for jobs again. His pool game didn't help that very much, and Marty knew that.

Lucy loved Val but was getting to the age where she might want to consider loving someone else. And Ty, the pro player seemed like he was triggering something inside of Lucy that made her want to forget Val. Ty had continued to befriend Lucy and she grew accustomed to that, in fact so much that she started to actually like it. Lucy was just torn between two choices: Val or go back to her family. She had time: though. For now they would play it by ear.

Val, on the other hand, had to make money, pay off his expenses, and also make enough to keep Lucy interested. There was also some incentive for Val to make a large and quick profit off something so that his mother could survive.

Val loved his mother, Esther. He didn't want to see her die in vain. Val was about to lose his mind, but something inside of him made him believe that with Jasper's help and guidance he would get through it, and everything would be fine.

The next morning Val woke up and noticed that Lucy was not home. Val and Lucy had talked to each other like a happily married couple for the longest time. They had, of course, stopped talking like they used to. Val missed Lucy's charm, and to the contrary, he missed charming her, smelling her perfume, gazing into those gorgeous blue eyes. Things had really gone to hell, but because Lucy wasn't home and the bed was disheveled and unmade, Val had to worry a little.

Val dialed her number quickly on his phone.

No answer. It went to voicemail. Val clicked End.

"Crap," Val said out loud.

Val took a quick shower, feeling the cold water splash against his face. His once filthy skin, covered in pool chalk, now was clean as a whistle; he looked sharper now. Val hopped out of the shower and slipped on his jean pants while he brushed his teeth. He got out of the bathroom and looked at his phone. She hadn't called him back or texted him yet.

Val sent her a text that said, "Where are you?"

Jasper was at his apartment organizing his money. He had put his winnings underneath his bed when he noticed something missing. Where was his stash? He had a stash of money in rubber bands hidden under his bed that was now not there.

"The landlord!" Jasper thought out loud. It was the landlord. It had to have been. No one else had access to the apartment and there was clearly no sign of a break in. Jasper checked the voicemail on the landline to see if anyone had called recently, and sure enough there was one missed call. It was Jason! Jason Burnen. It had to have been. He didn't think anyone else would have left him a voicemail. Jasper listened to it.

"Mister Slovansky, this is your landlord, Jason, I just want to inform you that you have two weeks to move out of the apartment, or we will get the police involved. I am giving you your two-week notice. Have a wonderful day!"

Jasper wasn't sure what to do. He was in debt to so many people, he just decided to deal with it on his own terms. It had finally caught up with him, and he had gotten the message. His life in the fast lane was ending. Jasper was learning his lesson, or was he?

Val was all he had left. Val was like a son to him, and without Val he meant nothing to anybody. Jasper was a zero, a degenerate who had been forced into this life and exploited by his own demons inside. The sport of billiards saw him as an outlier, a stranger who needed help.

"God help me!" Jasper said out loud.

Ty was hanging out at the bar that night, sitting right next to Lucy when Val walked in.

Val just decided to remain perfectly composed in this situation and not overreact. Ty was sitting next to Lucy, and they were relaxing, drinking, and talking casually. Val sat down next to Lucy on the chair next to her.

"What have you been up to?" Lucy asked Val.

"I've been working on getting our lives back together."

Ty, quite rudely, interrupted and asked Val, "So… you've really upped your game I heard. I'd still love for you to join our team. What do ya say, Val?"

A moment of silence followed and then a sharp reply from Val, "Man, would you take a nap?"

Ty took the hint that Val didn't want to talk about leagues and remained quiet after that. Ty got up out of his seat and started hitting balls on the table next to the bar.

"Can I get you something to drink?" asked the bartender.

Val shook his head and looked over at Lucy. Lucy looked back at him and said nothing.

Shortly thereafter Jasper walked in holding a bottle of Corona. He stopped near the entrance and took a huge gulp of it. Then he threw it in the nearby trash can. He was eyeballing Ty as he hit balls. He was also taking in Val and Lucy sitting at the bar counter. He was trying to come across as sober, but it wasn't working very well. In reality, Jasper had only had one beer, but acted like he had just hit his last. That was just how he was and how he wanted it, too. It was his protection from the crowd's opinion and the hype of himself.

Ty, after hitting a few balls and noticing Jasper, walked over to Lucy and Val. For the first time in forever, Jasper said something to try to antagonize Ty. It wasn't that he disliked Ty. It was more a matter of business. It was about the business of betting and pool, and nothing personal, either. He was also sticking up for Val, because he knew that they wanted to be left alone.

"Sly Ty, Val knows your league ain't for him now, so buzz off!"

"Hey, man, good things happen to good players…" Ty retorted.

"We'll see about that. How much of a betting man are ya?" Jasper spun the statement. Ty stopped hitting balls suddenly and looked over at him for once, making eye contact.

"What do you want to do, old man? I've got till the crack of dawn… hehe."

"Oh do you now? Well at my age I ain't got the stamina for that, but you can bet my boy Val here does. Val?" Jasper whistled loudly over to Val.

"Your boy? Okay, bring it!" Ty challenged.

Ty and Val made eye contact. Val got up out of his seat next to Lucy and said to her, "I'll be right back!"

Jasper and Val talked, standing just far enough so Ty couldn't hear them.

"I think you can take him, kid. Just remember what I taught you. Stay focused… don't sweat the score, and don't think about who you are playing. Play the table, okay, kid?"

"The guy's a freaking pro… Should I ask for weight?"

"Yes, of course you should. But don't be scared to play him even, either. Make him an offer. If he doesn't give up the weight, just play him straight even. You've got no choice at this point." Jasper whispered quietly.

"Okay, okay, I got this. I'm gonna try and bust him!"

Ty slammed a 9-ball into the corner pocket and said to Val, "I'll play you for anything you want, for as long as you want, wherever you want, sir!"

"What you giving up?" Val asked as he carried his cue case over to the table. He set it on the table next to one of the corner pockets and started to pull out his cues one at a time. He assembled them slowly.

A moment of silence ensued while Ty considered what fair game was. Jasper sat down at a table at a distance getting ready to observe what was to follow.

"I can't give you weight, as often as you play…. You're already a champion, winning tournaments all over. I know who you run with."

Val had just realized that his mentor had earned Ty's respect. In admitting that he knew who Val ran with, and that he couldn't possibly want to give him any spot, Ty had confessed to liking Jasper and his ways. This, in and of itself, was a victory for them, and they would have to take advantage of it.

They had agreed to play 9-ball, 100 dollars a game. Suddenly the whole room became quiet. Then a loud snap of the balls breaking echoed throughout the pool room. Boom! It was Val's break. His snap was completely on point. The wing ball dropped right away, and Val proceeded with the run out. He had no balls tied up. The 1-ball was in a tough spot to where he would have to cut the ball in. The shot was above average difficulty, and there weren't any obvious safeties on the table that he could think of at the time. His heart was beating fast.

Val stroked the cue ball and the 1-ball cruised into the pocket, but hung up right next to the corner. Val had missed his 1-ball shot. Ty quickly ran out the table until he got bad shape on his 7-ball. After contemplating the table for a minute, he decided to play safe and executed a defense that put Val in his place.

"It's only gonna get worse from here, buddy," Ty said as he put Val in what was called pool player's "jail." Val had no easy run-out. He was hooked, and the only shot he could see was a one-rail kick. Val studied the table and then stroked the ball in, nailing the kick shot. Swish!

"Oh yeah, for you it is. For you it's going to go downhill real fast!" Val said with a grin on his face. Val won the first game, making the rest of the easy run-out.

Val got down on his shot after the break and noticed something funny in his peripherals. It was Lucy and Ty sitting right next to each other on the side, observing him shoot. Val adjusted himself and got back up from the cue ball. He looked closer at Sly

Ty and saw that he was holding hands with Lucy. As Val moved the cue back and forth along his skinny fingers he noticed now Ty was rubbing Lucy's leg. *Was it a nightmare or was this really happening?*

Val decided he needed to go to the bathroom so he set his cue on the table.

"I'll be right back," he said as he stared them both down and walked over to the bathroom.

In the bathroom Val washed his hands and rubbed the sweat from his face. Val felt a shadow behind him.

It was Sly Ty.

"Hey Val, what you doing in here? Smoking a joint?"

Val at this point was so ticked off he could barely think, so he just decided to act. He grabbed Ty by the throat and slammed him against the wall. Ty screamed like a little girl.

"What the hell is wrong with you, man? Let me go, dude," Ty barely squeezed out of his vocals. Val finally let go of him and spoke.

"Look here buddy, I'm a clean player, alright? I don't smoke weed! And next time I see you rubbing Lucy's leg or doing whatever you're trying to do to her, there will be payback!"

So they both got back to the pool table, and Val finished his run-out. Ty, embarrassed like never before, quit after a few games. He simply set his cue case on the table and took apart his cue sticks.

"I've had enough drama with you, man. I'm finished. Here's three hundo… enjoy it!" Ty said, handing him the cash.

"I guess good things do happen to good players… Here's ten dollars so you can go buy yourself a sandwich!"

Val threw a ten-dollar bill on the table.

Ty blushed.

"I'll see you at the Tour!" Ty said.

Jasper smiled in the distance.

Jasper gave Val a fist pump.

"You're learning to freewheel with the best of them," Jasper said at a low tone so only Val could hear it.

"I gotta talk to Lucy."

Val quickly hustled over to his ex-girlfriend.

"So you found a new bestie I see?"

Lucy started to get teary-eyed.

"How could you do this to me? I can't have this!"

"I'm sorry, babe, I…" Lucy tried to explain but couldn't find the right words. It was over between them.

Val mustered the only ounce of love he had left for her and tried to hug her. She refused it and walked away very upset.

15

The next day Val slept around at the house. His ex had finally hit the road and left him. She mentioned she would be moving to her cousin Vicki's place if she was lucky. All it took was a little bit of explaining on Lucy's part to convince Vicki to allow it. Val knew he had made mistakes in life and deserved what he was getting quite naturally.

Val watched some pro pool as he ate a ham sandwich he had just made. Feeling nothing at all, he just sat there and chowed down on his luncheon when he suddenly received a very unexpected call from an anonymous number on his cell phone. Normally he didn't take calls, but he was in such a weird mood he just picked it up quite oblivious to the possible consequences.

"Hello, this is Val."

"Is this Val Madonna from the Saint Louis pool community?"

Val, feeling like the local celebrity, replied rather awkwardly.

"Yes, I'm a pool player. What can I do for you, sir?"

"This is Shooter Eddie with Shooter Eddie Cues and Cases, we are a pool vendor based out of Las Vegas, Nevada. I was hoping I could strike your fancy by offering you a spot as one of our touring pro players. Did you have a moment to talk?"

"How'd you hear of me? What kind of offer is this?"

"Well, a guy named Big Slick over there in Saint Louis seems to think pretty highly of you. We heard you have some business management experience and could use someone like you to help run the pool room we have over here in Vegas."

"Wow, well that is unbelievable, and yes, that does strike my fancy, sir. And you are correct, I did four years in Bloomington U and got my degree there. Been playing pool a long time. I've never been to Vegas."

"I will be in Saint Louis this week doing some work. We'd like to have you over for dinner if you have some time in the next few days. How does your schedule look?"

Val gave him the date of tomorrow for the meeting. When Val got off the phone with the guy he screamed like he had just hit the lottery for one million. Who was Shooter Eddie, and how did he know of the pool hall owner Big Slick? This was unbelievable. Val was overjoyed with happiness, and he wanted to tell everyone he knew.

This could be Val's big break, he pondered. He had dreamt for so long about hitting it big in the pool scene and now this! Somebody had actually acknowledged and officially recognized him as a player, and now it was his to lose. He could simply not mess this one up.

The next day it was snowing heavily. Val pulled up in his car to the sponsor's contact's house. Well, it was more than just a house. It was like a mini-mansion, one of those multi-story houses you rarely see with big white pillars and a beautiful, spacious front yard. And it looked beautiful in the white snow as it fell to the ground and accumulated along the grass in front. Val walked along the sidewalk with butterflies in his stomach not quite sure what to expect. He decided he would just be himself and let things happen.

Val rang the doorbell. A gentleman answered the door and appeared shortly after. The man wore cotton corduroy pants with a block-suede, long-sleeve sweatshirt, the kind you would only buy from a Nordstrom store, very expensive looking.

"Hello," Val spit out, not quite sure what to say exactly to this man of mystery. The man finally introduced himself after a moment of awkward silence.

"And you must be Val! I am Dave Sheffield. It is a pleasure to finally meet you!"

The man reached out,shook his hand, and welcomed him inside. Inside the house, the ceiling was decorated with magnificent chandeliers, and Val took it all in, cherishing this moment deeply.

Another individual appeared out of nowhere, dressed similarly to Dave but a lot taller and more muscular.

"Val! You must be the young gun, Val!" said the man as he walked towards him, reaching out his hand.

"Yes that's me. I'm Val," he said, laughing nervously.

"I'm Shooter Eddie, the founder of Shooter Cues and Cases. Really nice to meet you! We have a pool table in the basement. Would you like to come check it out?"

"Sure!" Val replied and followed them both downstairs.

"We have some other representatives from the company coming today for dinner. They just want to, you know, give you a warmest welcome and see if this is something you would like to pursue. No pressure!"

Val nodded his head and when they arrived in the basement, the setup was spectacular and homely. Val took a deep breath of air. He had just remembered that he didn't have his cues with him.

Shooter Eddie walked behind the basement bar, looking for something. Shooter then threw him a cue, and Val had to react quickly sohe grabbed it with both hands.

"What is this?" Val asked.

"This, my friend, is your Shooter Cue stick, and this…" Eddie grabbed another item from behind the counter and handed it to Val.

"… is your Shooter case. I hope you like it, Val. We designed that cue custom for your height and size. The length and weight should be perfect for you!"

Shooter Eddie then instructed Val to hit some balls, and try it out. Val complied and started hitting balls with it on their nine-foot table. The stick hit great. It was like feeling nothing at all on every shot.

The doorbell rang a few more times as the night went on. More company people came in. Downstairs, the room was crowded with people now, all hanging out and talking while Val hit balls with Shooter Eddie. Shooter Eddie seemed impressed.

"So the kid can play, huh? Got any trick shots?" a random person directed towards Val.

Val, looking tough, answered him. He had been practicing some pool tricks the other night.

"I got a few, yeah."

"Well, let's see them," replied another sponsor.

Val began to set up the shot that he planned to demonstrate to his audience. He was going to need every ball on the pool table. He was going to need fifteen balls and the cue ball, so he grabbed them all out of the pockets and started to set up the shot.

He first placed one ball about an inch away from the side pocket. Then he wired four sets of two balls together, frozen against the rail adjacent to the side pocket where the other ball was. Wired balls have no air or space between them and are touching. These balls were at an angle so that when the cue ball would strike it, the balls would separate and collide with each other a certain way, sending the last ball in that line down to the end rail, where Val had connected two sets of three balls wired to each other. The first set was wired so that when the object ball struck it, the third ball in that wired set would bounce off the bottom rail and hit the second set of three wired balls, where the 8-ball was. The 8-ball was supposed to ride the rail all the way up to the side pocket, and carom off the first ball he had set up an inch from the side pocket, and land in the pocket for the win. If Val could pull this off, he'd really impress these boys.

Val had everything set up the way he needed it. He got down on whitey and stroked the ball while aiming very low with a power stroke. The balls frozen against the rail reacted and separated like fireworks. Balls moved about everywhere, in every direction on the table. The 8-ball cruised up table in the middle of all this and bounced off the ball into the side pocket.

He had done it!

"Got yourself a real player here, Shooter Eddie! And what do ya call that trick shot, Val?" Dave asked.

"It's called the Around the World Shot."

Later on that evening, Val and the gang had dinner together. Shooter and Dave were the main guys that did most of the talking with Val. Once the dinner was prepared and Dave served everyone their plates, Shooter stood up and had some words for the group.

"Everyone, I would like to welcome Val to the Shooter Cues and Cases organization. Val, if you would please stand up? Val is a great pool player, and he has some business experience. I think he will be a great addition to the team as one of our touring pros. He will also be helping out at the shop and pool room," said Shooter Eddie.

Shooter sat down, and Val followed suit. Much to Val's surprise, Shooter had asked him to say grace in front of everybody. It had caught him off guard completely.

"Well Val, I just wanted to say how I love watching you play pool, especially on my home table! Now, would you like to say grace for us?"

"Of course," Val said nervously.

Val stood up at the table. All eyes on him, in anticipation.

"Rub a dub dub… Thanks for the grub! Yay, God!"

All the sponsors smiled, and a few giggled and responded with, "Amen."

When Val got home, Lucy was gone. Lucy had packed her things and moved on with her life. Val called Jasper right away to tell him the news about where he would be for a while and what he would be doing. Val was almost certain Jasper would be happy for him. The conversation went well.

"I'm moving to Vegas, I'll be going back and forth for a while. I just wanted to let you know how much I appreciate everything you've done for my pool game," Val thanked him over the phone.

"Kid, you've got to stick to your guns, cause you're walking into a whole other league. I wish you the best, but just remember what I taught you, and you'll be fine. Where you're going there will be not much room for error."

Month after month went by, and Lucy hadn't heard from Val. They had officially been crossed out from each other's lives and were finished. Lucy wanted a second chance. She did, but Val wasn't being so forgiving. In fact, he was now living in Las Vegas working for his sponsor.

Pool wasn't all about money, though. Val just wanted to play the game that he loved and make enough money to get by. He still wanted to make enough money to save his mother so she could afford treatment. That meant that he would have to somehow make a lot of money in a short period of time. Winning the State Tour in Missouri was an option for him. There was also a big tournament in Las Vegas near the end of the year. If he could win one of these, he would have enough to pay for the treatment, her brain surgery, and he would be doing a great thing for his mother. As they say, parents take good care of their kids. Then when the kids grow up, it is their responsibility to take care of their parents.

At the bar in Saint Louis, Jasper was having a heart-to-heart with Lucy. Lucy and Jasper had a beverage and chatted together about Val.

"I'm sorry about Val," Jasper said with sympathy.

Lucy had explained how she had not been able to reach Val at all over the phone and was worried.

"I've been staying with my cousin Vicki. I can't believe I lost him."

"Lucy, you need to go see him. He has really changed. He's working with a guy in Las Vegas named Shooter Eddie. Company is Shooter Cues and Cases, Inc. They sponsor pool players like him. I hear he's doing great!"

Lucy was teary-eyed. She didn't know what to do or say to Jasper even. She was depressed over it and vulnerable to anyone who would take a little time to comfort her or show her some much-needed attention.

"I feel partly to blame for all this, Lucy. So... out of the goodness of my heart, I'm going to try to get you two back together."

"Oh my gosh, Jasper, that would be fantastic!! Would you really? I mean, would he forgive me for my infidelity? I feel horrible."

"Yes, he would forgive you. I'm no Dr. Phil, but I know Val well, and I'd say he's got enough of a heart for ya to give you another shot. Take my advice and go to him. Take a plane to Vegas and get your boyfriend back!"

Jasper slid three hundred-dollar bills across the bar towards Lucy.

"Take the money. Buy yourself a plane ticket and go!"

Lucy took the money and gave Jasper a kiss on the cheek. She then began to leave the bar and get her things.

16

It was the day of the tournament, both pros and semi-pros. It took place in a pool room in Vegas. The pool room was filled with players everywhere, and the crowd was lively but, at the same time, getting in good form for the tournament. Photographers took pictures. Pool vendors lined the walkways selling cues and raffling off various billiards paraphernalia. And pool players filled the tables amid the action. The LED lights reflected onto the pool tables a beautiful, crisp color of white. The smoke-free room looked splendid and lit with verve and exuberance.

Val had to admit the room was very nice and exquisite, and he had never seen so many pool tables in one room before. There were hundreds of Valley bar tables in about four different rooms in the Vegas Westgate HotelH.

Val had chosen to play in this tournament over the one in Missouri simply out of convenience. Both tournaments paid a lot, but since his sponsorship was providing an entry into the one in Vegas, this tournament was the better choice. This was where Val would begin to really thrive, he thought.

This tournament would be broadcasted live on television as well. With 128 players signed up, Jasper was tuned in watching it at the bar in Saint Louis with his buddy Lee. Lee wanted to bet on the matches, so Jasper obliged him.

"What makes you so sure about Val? I'll bet against him, but you gotta give me odds on the money since Val is obviously the favorite in this one," Lee explained.

"I've got a hunch. I'll give you a three-game spread. How's that? If Val wins nine to six, you win! So the other guy has to win six games."

Lee adjusted himself and spoke.

"How much you want to bet?"

"Make it five hundred."

"Deal!"

Lee smiled confidently. But Val broke the balls and made the one in the side off the break right away. He quickly ran out the rack with ease. Game one went to Val. Val proceeded to win game after game, and his opponent didn't get a chance at the table until the fourth rack.

Val ended up winning his first round nine to thre, making Jasper 500 dollars richer.

Jasper got excited.

"This man knows too much here. He knows too much. That young gun can shoot a lick, oh boy, he's hot right now!" Lee said walking around in circles sounding frustrated with himself.

Jasper smiled and took his winnings. Jasper went home that night to watch the rest of the tournament there. On his drive home he received an anonymous text message. It was from one of his neighbors. His name was Tom, and he was on the neighborhood watch team. Tom's message warned Jasper that there was a man at his door that looked a little shady. Jasper just decided to shrug it off and have a beer.

At his apartment, he grabbed a Bud Light and sat to rest on the couch. He turned on the TV to spectate the rest of the Vegas tournament. As he watched, he thought about what he had done for Val, and how things had worked out for him. Jasper was exceedingly happy for his apprentice and proud of himself for what he had done for the youngster.

Jasper, maybe a little too content with himself, went to the fridge to grab another adult beverage. He then grabbed another and another until he was completely wasted on his couch.

Listening to the radio, Vincent was speeding like a demon down the highway while Don Henley blared. He puffed a cigarette and flicked it out the window after he was done with it. Its spark hit the pavement and left a streak of red on the road behind him.

He got off the highway and pulled into the subdivision where Jasper lived.

"On table thirty-nine we have Wiley Brunson and Val Madonna," announced the tournament director over the microphone.

Val hurried right away over to table thirty-nine. He waited for his opponent there. Wiley had a broken cue tip that needed fixing, so Val had to wait a little longer than normal. The director allowed him to get his tip fixed by one of the nearby vendors.

Wiley finally got over to the table and reached out to shake Val's hand, introducing himself.

"I'm Wiley!"

Wiley was an old school pro player. He had been playing pool a long time, going on sixty years. He had been playing his whole life, too. Val would try to do his best, though.

This was the fourth-round match. If Val won this one, he would for sure be in the money rounds.

The match went back and forth, back and forth. Val won a game, and then Wiley won one.

It ended up being hill-hill. And it was Wiley's break.

Wiley broke with all his strength and ran, knocking Val into the loser's bracket. It was the ideal break for Wiley to run out, all the balls spread perfectly about the table. At that point, Val felt like he still had enough mental strength to make it to the money rounds. He would have to win his next one for sure.

As Jasper sat on his sofa at home, he took a long gulp beer when he suddenly heard a loud thud. He got up to find out what it was. It sounded at first like a subway train. But when he got up and started walking, it got louder as he got closer to it. Now it sounded like a gunshot.

Boom!

Boom!

Boom!

The sound was in intervals of three, three beats at a time. Jasper still wasn't sure what it was. He looked out the window, beer in hand, and saw nothing but the usual: a cloudless night sky and his front yard.

Jasper, in his attempt to somehow maintain his sobriety, just realized that it might not be a train, or a plane, or anything quite like that. It was, in reality, a man knocking on his front door. So he walked over to the front door.

"Who is it?" he yelled.

Nothing but loud thuds.

Boom!

Boom!

"Who is there?" Jasper inquired again, louder this time. Jasper mused for a moment, nearly fell over, deep in thought and trying to catch a glimpse out the window of whomever was outside his door without him noticing.

Jasper opened the door to see his landlord. It was Jason, and he didn't look happy. Jason wanted him gone, so Jasper obliged him. Hardly any words had to be said. Jasper already knew. He already started gathering his belongings. Time was up. And now he would have to find a new place to live. The first thing he looked for was the stash under his bed. He got down on his knees and reached underneath, but felt nothing. He reached a little further. Still nothing. Finally, now utterly convinced that something was off, he grabbed a flashlight and peeked under the bed. Nothing there. Jasper knew the time was up for his games.

In Vegas, Val was at the pool room getting ready, getting in stroke for his next match. It was 12 AM. His eyeballs were about to fall out of their sockets, but doing what he loved, it didn't matter that much to him. Suddenly, he heard a familiar voice from behind him.

"What, can't you make a ball?" said a familiar female voice as he missed a shot. Val turned around surprised.

"Lucy?"

"Where have you been hiding out, stranger?"

"Well I don't think I need to answer that. Hehe. So you flew here just for me? What's your story, Lucy? I thought we were through?"

"No, Val, I flew here because I love penny slots. Yes, for you!"

Lucy blushed and seemed a little aggravated by the question.

They hugged.

Lucy asked the million-dollar question.

"Can you forgive me?"

Val hesitated and leaned forward. His body was right next to hers now. They were chest to chest. Val tried to give her a kiss and missed, so he kissed her on the cheek instead.

Val nodded his head. They called his next match on the microphone.

"Well, I think you've got a match. I'll be watching you from the stands, Val. Go kick some butt!"

Before leaving, Lucy told Val that she loved him.

Val ended up playing Sly Ty for the final match. The crowd was intensely spectating the match. Lucy was in the audience now. Val took a seat and grabbed some water while Ty was shooting. The score was one to one. Ty won the next game, making it two to one.

Ty broke the balls up again, and the Aramith cue ball flew up in the air a couple feet and landed back on the table. Ty had a tough bank shot on the 1-ball that he missed.

Val took another gulp of water at his chair and set the glass down. He rose from his seat and approached the pool table.

Val had an easy run-out from there and won that game. The score was now two to two.

In a race to nine, Ty ran a few racks and ended up getting to the hill game while Val was still only at two games won. The score was now eight to two, in Ty's favor.

It was now Val's break, and before he broke, he looked over at the camera person running the stream for their match up. He thought of his mother Esther and her illness. Val wanted to say something in the camera because he knew his mother was watching. He wanted to touch home, so he looked straight into the lens of the camera.

"I love you, Mom! I'll be home after this pool tournament!"

He took a deep breath of air and looked over at Ty who was sitting in his seat in bewilderment and awe. He asked Ty if he was ready for him to start playing, rhetorically. Ty reacted with little emotion and waved to the table, signaling him to resume the match as normal.

Val ran multiple racks and ended up tying the match up at eight to eight.

Val and Ty got into a safety duel after Val's break on the hill-hill match.

Ty hooked Val on the 7-ball. The cue ball was trapped frozen between the cushion and the 8-ball. The 7-ball was sitting in the corner pocket and the 9-ball was in the open, too. Val had only one shot that he saw on the table. It was a three-rail kick for the win. Val did a 360, circling the table while he inspected everything. He lined his cue up on the table using the diamond system. The diamond system was a system for making kicks and banks that involved counting points on the rails, simple mathematical formulas, and parallel shifts.

Someone in the audience yelled out to Val.

"You got this, kid!!"

Val aimed into the cushion with a touch of right-hand English. The cue ball traveled three rails and sank the 7-ball in. The cue ball rested in the corner pocket where the 7-ball was potted.

Now all he had was a bank shot, and he would win!

Val lined up the bank and could really feel the pressure on him now.

Val stroked whitey. The ball rolled forward and collided with the 9-ball. The 9-ball bounced off the cushion and made its way to the destination. It was heading straight into the side pocket and it did. Ball potted and match won!

Ty walked over to Val. Val jumped up on the pool table before Ty could get there. He held his cue in his hands as he yelled in excitement on top of the table.

"Get down here so I can shake your hand, Val. You got me again. Nice match!"

"Good game, Ty! Thanks!"

Ty and Val shook hands after Val lowered himself back to ground level.

The tournament director along with Val's sponsors all came rushing over to the table with a trophy to hand him.

"And the winner of the Vegas 9-ball Open this year is Val Madonna from Saint Louis, MO. He will be taking home twenty-five thousand dollars. And second place goes to Ty Dino! Congratulations to the winners!"

"Congratulations, Val!" Shooter Eddie reached over to fist bump him. Everyone was happy for him and excited. The room was filled with energy. Lucy came over to him and gave him a hard kiss. They were in love again. Val smelt her perfume and her womanly touch as they kissed in front of the entire room. There was truly magic in the air that night. Val was relieved and wanted to go talk to Esther about her treatment. He needed to get this cash over to her aid as soon as humanly possible.

Val held up the trophy standing next to Lucy while they took a picture of him and her. He had a big smile on his face while Lucy kissed him on the cheek...

In the Vegas hotel, Val and Lucy raced down the hall toward the elevator. They had made up finally, and now it was their chance to celebrate. They giggled together as they made it into their hotel room, making fun of each other, particularly Val's jumping on the pool table in excitement. Lucy thought that was hysterical but adorable at the same time. Suddenly, they both stopped laughing as they came to a halt inside the room Lucy gave him a stern look, and Val returned it, staring back. Val wanted to give Lucy what she had been waiting so patiently for: a good time and a reason to stay with him for the rest of their lives. So Val, knowing he had already won her over, approached her face to face and held the back of her head with his hand, stroking her hair between his finger tips. He gave her a soft kiss on the cheek and she then immediately started to take his jean pants off for him, loosening the buckle. The jeans fell to the floor as they made love vigorously. Lucy and Val did the dirty deed together for the first time in a long, long time and enjoyed it passionately. They had been together before, but this time it was extra special to them. Val and Lucy crashed into bed and fell asleep together.

In the morning Val woke up with a cramp in his thigh. He crawled out of bed and got dressed, slipping on a brand new pair of jeans while smiling at Lucy as she slept through the morning. Val pulled out his laptop and started typing. He was looking for an airline fare back to Saint Louis. He needed to do what must be done for his Mom. He scanned through the internet and checked for air fares from various airlines. He found one for late that day and took it directly to Saint Louis. He was headed home with Lucy, but would be back.

That afternoon, after the plane landed, Val and Lucy had settled back into their home together. He grabbed some money from out of his drawer where he had kept it and counted it. He wanted to make sure he had at least fifteen thousand dollars. Val carefully placed the Benjamins in stacks of ten. He added them up as he laid them on his bed. They added up to twenty-three thousand dollars! He was overjoyed.

With deep pockets full of cash, Val walked with a sense of due diligence and urgency into Mercy Hospital where his mother was resting after the surgery had taken place. He truly wanted to help his mother pay off the medical bill for the surgery, but needed to get to the hospital and talk to his mother first. The hospital smelled funny. All hospitals have that wretched aroma anyway. As he walked briskly through the hallways of the building, he kept peeking through each room, thinking of his mother as he looked inside at the various hospital patients. He had witnessed a few people sobbing in there. None of them were truly his beloved mom, of course. He kept on walking, until he made it to room 453 on the fourth floor. That was the room the receptionist had said she was in.

Val walked in and saw his mother. She had her eyes closed, but the up-and-down motion of her stomach indicated life. Val sat down in the chair next to her bed and gently held her arm with his hand. Her eyes opened and she turned her head slightly to her son.

"Hey, Val," Esther said.

"Mom... how you doing?"

"Well, let's just say that the surgeon is a miracle worker."

"So, they did it?"

"Yes, it was a success! Your prayers were answered, son!"

Val had tears of happiness. Tears ran down his face, and before Esther could say or do anything, Val got up out of his chair, pacing around the room. The doctor came in, knocking on the door at that time. Seeing Val he nodded and smiled at him. The two of them walked outside and talked about his mother's health. The doctor told Val it was a successful surgery. All went well, and they were lucky to have discovered the cancer at the early stage it was in, before it had spread to other parts of her brain. Val couldn't have been happier knowing that she was going to be okay.

He sat back down with his mother.

"Son, before I went into surgery, it hit me that we never discussed your father much. Well, I wanted you to know that you are starting to remind me of him a lot. In case I never told you, his name was Louie." Esther spoke with a sharp, raspy voice, but a quiet tone, as if delivering a very important message, and it was significant between the two of them.

Val put his hand over his mouth, and he looked like he had just seen a ghost as he looked at the photograph that his mother had handed him. He felt an overwhelming sense of relief. His mother had kept it a secret. Why? Val supposed that his friends and family must have truly cared for him. He laughed to himself as he kept staring at the beautiful picture of his father. He was a little overwhelmed and, at the same time, shocked. Esther feared for Val just as his friends did. She feared for the exposure he was getting to the dangers of pool hustling. She feared for his life. Now, she had clearly felt like Val needed to wake up to his true calling. She believed in Val and trusted her son to follow his passion in life. Val deserved to know the truth about his father.

The picture was of a middle-aged man holding a Meucci cue with an open bridge on the table and hands slightly contracted in preparing his stroke. He had long, bushy, brown hair. A crowd of people observed behind him. On the backside of the photo, a caption read Saint Louie Louie Roberts.

Val tucked the photo into his jacket pocket, sat up and gave his mother a soft kiss on the cheek as he handed her fifteen thousand dollars in cash.

"I told you I'd be back to help you out!" Val uttered softly. "Love you, Mom!"

Mrs. Madonna smiled pleasantly and discreetly handed the money back to him and said, "Just keep that for now."

He turned around to see the smiling faces of Lucy and Marty. They both looked relieved. The mood was very serene in the hospital that night. Lucy and Marty had few words to say. Val hadn't expected to see them there at that precise time, even though he did let them know where his mother was. The four of them hung out for a little while and then said their goodbyes. Shortly after, they all walked out of the hospital together. Later the next day, Mrs. Madonna was discharged from the hospital, when Val picked her up and got her settled back into her home.

17

A few years had gone by since Val had won the tournament in Vegas and sealed his sponsorship with Shooter Cues. It was March, 2019. In Barnhart, Missouri, there was a pool room and bar known as Kenny's Bar and Grill just south of Saint Louis where all the action was. Val started hanging out there quite a bit with Lucy and Marty. Kenny's was divided in two sections: a pool room filled with hustlers and pool hall junkies, and a full bar scene with a stage for bands, karaoke, and a dance floor. A lot of big shots played out of there, including Val and also a gentleman nicknamed Spider. He was in his late forties, bald and had a goatee. The Spider was a much-feared player in the pool scene, but not for his abilities. He was one of the best players around, nobody would doubt, but that's not what most players feared playing him for. It was about the way that he intimidated people as he moved around the table, and the way he got in good games all the time. The guy had more lines than a savvy car salesman. He had a line for just about everybody he knew and if he didn't know you and you liked to gamble, he would find a way to get to know you and gamble with you. Not too many people called the Spider by his first and last name. Not too many even knew his real name. When people talked about the Spider they referred to him as the Spider and only the Spider. When they talked to him to his face, they also called him the Spider. Spider was also one of the most brilliant locksmiths in the country. He only played when and if he had the dead nuts to win the game. He hardly ever got in a game he wasn't the favorite to win, which was another part of what made him so feared. Val tried to stay clear of players like him.

"Hey Spider, what you want to do for a dime or two? I bet I got more dimes than you got pennies, man!" Deon Williams woofed at the Spider as he shot with a young eleven year old who kept getting flustered after losing game after game to him. That was common among young crowds when they played the Spider. The Spider was just making a point with this youngster though, and the punchline was about to be delivered as the Spider looked over at Deon and spoke at a low volume to him.

"The kid's got to learn something," the Spider said to the man smiling.

The youngster slammed his cue on the table and racked the balls up vigorously. A few players observed as the Spider ran over the youngster, winning every game. Most of the older crowd understood the point that the Spider was making. Spider and the kid weren't playing for anything. It was harmless, and nobody was hurt.

Corey was the little guy's name, and he did not look so happy. The thing was, the Spider would never make a point like this unless it was worth making. Corey was a youngster with immense talent at pool. His ball-making skills were better than anyone his age. He had potential to be a world champion. Already snapping off small tournaments, this kid was fun to watch at his age.

The Spider made his way over to the youngster and reached out to shake Corey's hand. He reluctantly shook his hand, and before the Spider could walk away, Corey said something quietly, almost imperceptibly. The Spider turned back around.

"Um, what was that?"

"You got lucky," Corey said, frowning.

"Twenty-five games in a row!?" he retorted.

"It was fifteen."

The Spider laughed.

"Kid, you gotta learn to control your temper. You can't get so mad! If you keep doing that, you'll never develop any composure. You just can't win like that, alright?"

In pool, there is a fine line between getting angry and frustrated over missing balls, and playing angry. Anger in pool is okay, but you must learn to stay composed. If you can learn to harness and control your anger, you can, in a sense, increase your competitive edge, and thus shoot better. You see young guys slam their cues on the table in disappointment over missed shots. This will do nothing but release the energy you should be saving for the table. Playing with controlled anger is alright, but getting and acting angry over missed shots will only make your opponents feel more relaxed and less intimidated by you.

Corey frowned, hesitated, and then nodded. And that was it. The Spider had delivered his point. People respected the Spider for things like that. It was one of his talents in the pool world. The Spider was smart about people, especially young folks. Not everyone had the guts to do or say the things he had said all the time. The Spider did show a great consistency in his abilities. People liked him for his clout.

"So what can we play, Spider?" Deon repeated.

The Spider smiled like he had just caught his prey.

"Let's play some one pocket. Twenty-five a game?"

"Bring it on, man!" Deon said confidently.

Before they could get started, the Spider got a phone call from a Las Vegas area code. He warned Deon that it might be a minute before they played as he walked outside the bar. He picked up and said hello.

"This is Shooter. How you doing, Spider?"

"I'm alright, and yourself?"

"I have a proposition for you," Shooter said. Spider crossed his arms and grinned in silence.

"I need you to help me out. I got this player I'm backing, his name is Val Madonna. He's never played one pocket, but he plays a hell of a 9-ball game. I want him to learn how to play one pocket before he gets too old. Can you get him some help? "

Spider didn't have the extra time to mentor anybody, but would be happy to help in any way that he could. Spider was well connected, and he had heard of Val before. So, this would be easy for him. Spider agreed to help and hung up the phone.

Val was twenty-five years old now, and had grown his hair out like his father, Louie. *Louie Roberts was Val's father?* It was very hard to believe, he had thought to himself. How could it be? Val thought about this as he drove in his brand new 2019 Chevy Impala, he had just recently bought. Upon running over a pothole in the road, he nearly spilled his Styrofoam to-go cup filled with Pepsi as he drove down the highway on the way back home from a pool outing in Belle, MO. A few particles of soda spilled out and landed on the carpeting. Val noticed it and slowed the vehicle down a bit while clutching his drink firmly.

After winning that big tournament at the Westgate Hotel in Las Vegas, he had embarked on a very arduous journey. In the pool world, pros either made dough or they barely scathed by. And right now Val was just content. His mother, Esther, had already made her point, and Val had chosen his path. As a professional player, it was tough to make a living, and you had to always be on top of your game.

Esther, in an odd sort of way, wanted something else for Val. But in telling Val the truth about his father being a professional pool player, a legend, a man whose disappearance was surrounded by mystery, Val was determined to discover the truth behind his fate and continue his pro pool endeavors. Even though Esther wanted a different life for her beloved son, she wasn't afraid to finally reveal the truth about his father's history of being a pro pool player. It intrigued him that his own father was so much like himself. Val was very curious about this, and so he tried to do all that he could do to find answers behind the facts of his death, all to no avail. If his father was a legendary player, what could that mean for him? Would he start to play pool better soon at the level he was at?

As he drove down the highway, he considered these things among others. Val no longer lived in Vegas, but still had Shooter as his official sponsor. Val had moved back to Saint Louis at the beginning of the year to be closer to Lucy and her family who also lived in Missouri. Shooter agreed to remain his sponsor if he could produce wins. He had hired Dave Sheffield, his contact who lived in Saint Louis, to be Val's representative there, since Shooter lived in Vegas. Over the past few years, he had matched up with other pro players to play for thousands of dollars, winning most of the time but struggling in the pro tournaments. Val played mostly 9-ball sets, and 9-ball and 8-ball tournaments. He needed to learn a new game; his sponsor kept telling him. Even though Val could run racks, he needed to learn the safeties, the strategy better in 9-ball to take his game to the next level.

The pressure was really on him now since he only had one source of income. He needed to find a part-time job, he thought to himself. Val didn't like all this heat from Shooter and Dave to win tournaments. *These pro events were tough!*

Lucy had agreed to support Val from here on out, regardless of anything or anyone that would get in their way. Val had almost let another pro player steal her from him. They had talked and agreed that this would not happen again.

The phone rang, and Val picked it up. It was Lucy.

"Hey, babe!"

"I'm cooking dinner for us, babe. Are you coming home soon?"

Val smiled through the phone as he replied.

"Already on the way! Be home in about a half an hour or less!"

As Val drove, he sipped on his Pepsi. The highway got narrower as he drove towards his home in Saint Louis all the way from the boondocks of Belle, MO.

Val made small talk with Lucy over the phone for a little bit on his drive home. He had been in a pool room in Belle, Missouri where there was some action going on. He made a little money on the side there every now and then with some of the locals.

After arriving at his home, Val had dinner with Lucy. She had made him some sort of shredded chicken recipe she had discovered from one of her girlfriends. It turned out to be exquisitely tasty. Val complimented Lucy for making such a great meal. They were a happy couple again.

That night, before going to bed, Val did a google search on his laptop computer. He had been wondering about Louie and had been wanting to look up his obituary online. He didn't find anything. He would need to dig further as he could find nothing of substance regarding an obituary on his deceased father. Val went to sleep next to Lucy, while Lucy stayed up late reading a book.

18

Val had not seen his mother since she had recovered from her surgery, and was a little bit shaky to be seeing her and getting the opportunity to discuss the matter of his father. After finding out that his father was indeed, Louie Roberts, he needed some time to think and collect his thoughts, not to mention space from his mother. Val hopped out of the Impala that he drove in and walked up to the house. He took a deep breath of fresh air and rang the doorbell twice before she came to the door and opened it. Mrs. Madonna looked like she had aged. Her skin was starting to wrinkle a little more, but she retained a lot of her beauty.

"Come on in, Val," she said quietly. Once he stepped inside, they embraced each other.

"You want some water?" Esther said. Val nodded his head in agreement, but felt a little intimidated as well. They both sat down on the sofa.

"So, tell me, how are you and Lucy doing?"

"We are doing great. We have had some rough times, but all is good now. She's still working hard and seems happy to me."

Val drank a sip of his water as the conversation paused for a while, and Esther just smiled in comprehension of his statement. She understood.

"I suppose it's time that I tell you the truth about how your father died. A lot of people aren't sure how he passed away," she explained fighting back the emotions. "It was ruled a suicide, but everyone knows Louie didn't like guns, much less pulling the trigger. No gunpowder was found on his hands, either. Even though I wasn't with your father long, I knew Louie better than anyone. I know that he would have never done that."

Val wanted to delve deeper into the life of Louie, but at the same time he didn't. He leaned back on the sofa and tried to get comfortable while Esther talked.

"So, if he was so great, why not stay with him? Why let him leave you?"

"He didn't leave me intentionally, hon. Somebody killed him. Val, your father was a US Open Champion. In 1979, he won the US Open! You have some pretty big shoes to fill, son, if you ask me!"

Val's mom giggled as she said this and in response, Val blushed and felt almost humored by the talk—but he couldn't be. He was old enough to know the truth now. It was time that he became the man he was meant to be. He was meant to make a living playing pool for the rest of his life, and Mrs. Madonna was finally letting her son go. It was a beautiful, yet sort of sad moment, and Val was just soaking it all in. Val inquired further about the death.

"How did he get killed, and what happened?"

"A man named Andrew Stephens shot and killed him with a pistol."

"Why?" Val had asked with tears in his eyes.

"Andrew was in with the wrong people in his young life. He did a lot of bad drugs like cocaine and meth, but I think the reason that he decided to do what he did had to do with his envy of Louie's pool game. Andrew was definitely a jealous type, and when Louie won the US Open 9-ball event, there was nothing holding Andrew back from acting on his emotions. Andrew's dad helped direct the US Open events in Las Vegas where the pros play and sponsored a lot of pro players. Louie and Andrew used to be friends, until Louie got so serious about pool and turned into a pro. Today, I think Andrew is moving his way up in the world of billiards and becoming a pretty hot stick."

Val sank in his chair as the words came out and the story unfolded. Val had dedicated his life to pool, but now this was about more than pool; it was about getting even for his mother and himself. He wanted so desperately to get the justice they both deserved.

"How do you know all this, Mother? Is there any proof?"

"I know because I know Louie was not depressed, and he hated guns, like I said. He hated the mere sight of a gun. Andrew's father, Michael Stephens, was a great man and a great advocate of the pool world. Unfortunately, he let his son get messed up with some bad people. Years ago, at the funeral, Michael and I had a talk about Louie, and Michael gave me the lead into his own son —that was when I hired a private investigator."

A moment of silence ensued after Val had heard what he had wanted to hear.

"I love you, Mom!" Val exclaimed, getting out of his seat finally after a lengthy moment of silence.

"I love you too, son."

And that was the end of their conversation that night. They hugged. Not a lot more had to be said. Val took the time he had spent with his mother that night as consent to proceed with a life of pool. Professional pool was tough, but Val thought with this approval and little bit of inspiration from his mother, he could do great things for the pool world and succeed in life. Val drove home to resume his life with Lucy with a clearer understanding of his past and what his future could bring.

Across town in a pool room known as Cue and Cushion, the Freezer, Scott Frost, was truly a pleasure to watch play and a class act on and off the pool table. He had earned his props over the years and as an official Hall of Fame, one-pocket player, he was a spectacular player. Not only was he fun to watch but also intimidating to play with for money. Scott was already a true legend of the sport of billiards. When he got in stroke, Scott liked to use a long bridge, meaning the distance between his bridge hand and the tip was elongated. This was very typical among most professional players, though.

He had come to visit Saint Louis to put on exhibitions for $125.00 a lesson per player in a group session. The audience loved him as he showed them various one-hole shots. He let them practice each shot and explained how each was used, lining up each ball where it should be.

Most pool players know one pocket as a game of chess, figuratively speaking. Each player claims one hole to shoot at, either the bottom left or bottom right corner pocket. The game is beautiful and fun to play but slow to observe at times, because there is a lot of back-and-forth, safety sparring and jockeying for position, which can fatigue the mind and the eyes. You must know how to bank well to play one pocket also. Most would agree that if you can't bank well, you can't be a very good one pocket player.

At Cue and Cushion in the town of Overland, MO, one pocket was the game of choice for just about every local player that played out of there. At Cue and Cushion, they housed mainly nine-foot tables, a wide variety of them, too. They had one diamond table, also a nine footer, among several other brands like Gold Crown and Brunswick. Scott Frost, the Freezer, was putting on an exhibition there today, and that was the first time that Val had seen Scott. Val was hitting balls there, practicing when he first noticed the Freezer.

The Freezer wore a blue collared T-shirt and jeans. He was very tall and pretty good looking, too. He had a way with people in the pool world, and that was just another reason they loved learning from him.

Val stopped hitting balls suddenly, set his cue down, and walked over to the exhibition. The Freezer spoke loudly and deliberately as he instructed the pool students. It was fun to observe, but the Freezer didn't particularly like it when players freeloaded on his lessons which were supposed to be paid-for. One of the pool players in the audience, named Sherman, spoke up with a question.

"I gotta question, Scott. On banks, how do you tell if there is going to be a double hit?"

"Well, it's really a feel thing. You just gotta know it through experience. The more of those types of shots you hit, the better you'll be able to tell if there is going to be a double hit. What's your name, again?"

"I'm Sherman, but you can call me the Sherminator. That's my nickname," Sherman replied, and everyone around him just chuckled. Scott smiled wickedly and everyone could tell he liked the nickname.

Bank shots are a very important part of playing one pocket, and the double hit is when the cue ball intercepts the object ball on its way to the intended pocket after a bank off of a rail. Obviously, this is not a good thing for the shooter because it a lot of times will leave the other player a shot at his hole, not to mention they lose control of the cue ball. The Sherminator had posed a great question for the Freezer.

Val stood right next to Sherman and spoke at a low volume as not to interrupt the session.

"Good question… hey, who is this guy, anyway? Never seen him before."

"Scott Frost, the Freezer. He's a Hall of Fame, one-pocket player from Arizona, and he's giving out lessons."

Val looked like he had been satisfied to an extent, but still wanted to learn more about this guy. It was a rarity to see a legend of the game in a local pool room in Saint Louis. Val soon realized that he was not welcome in the session since he didn't pay Scott. Val went back to his table and observed from a distance while he ran racks in 9-ball.

Val recalled the lessons Jasper had given him years ago in ball making and shape playing; muscle movement memory was critical. Muscle movement memory was what some people would refer to as the pendulum motion of your arm when stroking the cue ball. Each pump stroke should be identical in form and movement, so that your aim is consistent.

The table Val was playing on was very well built and maintained to perfection. The pocket size was ideal for his skill level. The balls dropped in like butter on bread, and when he cut a ball in, most people couldn't cut that thin if they had a pair of scissors. That's how he felt tonight, freestyling in 9-ball, letting his stroke out on the nine-foot Brunswick. It felt natural, like he had just learned how to play the game. It was easy, and he made few mistakes.

The model of this table, very old in style of course, didn't do justice to the cloth and rails that played very smooth like glass. The table played phenomenally, and it wasn't like he was playing the table. The table played him, he thought to himself. Nothing could go wrong tonight. What a perfect and uninhibited evening of pool. Nights like that didn't come too often. It felt good to find a rhythm on a dream table and just let it out and let loose. It's good to experience good and bad, and if he had ever felt so distracted and off balance before playing pool, tonight had to be the other side of that coin.

The Freezer decided to walk over to him during his routine break from the lessons he was giving. He had already recognized Val as a strong player, possibly pro level. So he walked over and spoke to him. Scott extended his hand and introduced himself.

"I'm Scott, and you must be one of the local pros around here."

"My name is Val. Nice to meet you, Scott."

Val was a little overwhelmed to have met a Hall of Famed player. He really didn't know what to say to him exactly.

"Good to have met ya, too. I just wanted to introduce myself because I heard you shoot a pretty strong game of 9-ball. You ever thought about getting more into one pocket?"

"Yes, of course I have."

"Well, I'm going to be here the rest of this week and until Sunday. Then I'm headed back home to Arizona," Scott explained.

Val did want to learn the ways of one pocket. It was just a tough game to learn. It would take time, but he knew it would help his overall game. Val got Scott's phone number and continued shooting.

At the close of the evening, when the players were racking the balls up and preparing to head home to their families, Val followed suit.

The night swept over them, and the pool room became quieter, more empty now. Val packed up his Shooter cue and his Predator break stick and hustled over to the front desk where he was greeted by a friendly, dark-skinned man. He handed the man at the desk a 100 dollar bill for his pool time, asking for change.

"Son, where I come from, that IS change," he replied and Val laughed in response.

19

Andrew Stephens smoked a blunt in a Saint Louis alley just outside Biggie's restaurant with some of his friends, Gary and the Bear. They cracked jokes as Andrew smoked and handed the blunt off to Gary, who puffed the joint, and then after a while, handed it off to the Bear. He took the blunt from Gary forcefully and spoke.

"Sharing is caring, huh, boys?" the Bear muttered as he coughed like he had never done a roll before. The other two laughed at this and nodded their heads.

"Hey, Gary, why do we call 'em that anyway? The Bear? Why does Brady get that nickname?" Andrew asked. Brady looked insulted by this as Gary responded reluctantly.

"Well, don't ya remember what happened over in Minnesota, that bear that looked like it was gonna attack us? Yeah, but then Brady stood up on his tippytoes and yelled ROAR!!! Scared the shit out of that bear, and he ran away. Saved us all! Haha."

The group of friends loved that story and the way that Gary told it. It was truly a remarkable story, not to mention a great nickname for Brady since he was so big like a bear and his last name sounded like a bear: Behrdin. Brady the Bear Behrdin was his name.

The three left the alleyway and walked back into the restaurant where they were greeted by their waitress. She looked like she was overworked this evening, and like she hadn't had much sleep the previous night. Her eyes had bags underneath them, and she strutted lackadaisically to greet them at the table. Biggies was the type of restaurant anyone could go to, and any time of day also. It had a full-service bar near the entrance with dinner tables spread out elsewhere. The three of them were sitting at one of the tables.

The waitress asked the three gentlemen what they each wanted to drink. The Bear ordered a Corona Lite, Andrew ordered a Budweiser, and Gary ordered a glass of water. The three sat in silence for a few minutes before the awkwardness was broken up finally by Gary.

"So, anyone hear about the guy trying to beat ol Mosconi's famous record run in straight pool?" Gary asked the group and looked around at the other two guys.

"I heard there's a player named John Schmidt trying to break it. You think he can do it?" Andrew replied looking skeptical. He was asking the obvious but difficult-to-answer question. He got no direct answer from Gary. So he looked over at the Bear and spoke.

"Well, what do you think Bear?"

"Willie Mosconi holds the record at five hundred plus balls. I think Mr. 400 has a shot. They don't call him Mr. 400 for no reason, do they, Andrew?" the Bear said rhetorically.

At this time, the cute but haggard-looking, brunette waitress came over to their table again. She refilled their beverages and took their food order. Andrew and Brady both ordered cheeseburgers and fries. Gary decided to go with the rib-eye steak special.

"Does anyone remember Louie Roberts?" Gary had asked the guys.

Andrew immediately looked up from his meal and shot Gary an evil stare. His eyes turned bloodshot, Gary noticed, or was that just his imagination? Either way, nobody had ever seen Andrew Stephens look at somebody with such hatred built up before. Gary asked again, the same question, and Andrew continued his stare before he finally spoke back to him.

"Why in the living hell do you care if I remember the incomparable Saint Louie Louie Roberts?" Andrew asked rather bluntly. His stomach churned inside and he found it hard to digest his food that he was eating.

The other two looked appalled, and maybe even a little disgusted by Andrew's reaction. The incomparable Louie was a legend in the game.

"Well there's this up-and-comer, a young player, I saw him over at Kenny's Bar and Grill the other night, in Barnhart, MO. I noticed he played with a cue that had "Louie Roberts" etched, sort of engraved in it near the shaft. He shot a damn good stick. Any idea who this kid might be?"

Andrew stood up and excused himself from the table. He went to the bathroom and splashed water on his face a couple times. He then pulled out a box of cigarettes and a lighter. He grabbed one of the butts and placed it in between his lips. He then looked in the mirror and said out loud, "I didn't know Louie had a kid..."

Deon spoke with Vincent about Jasper that evening at Hot Shots bar in Webster. They conversed at the dinner table while they ate. The mood was very upbeat and the jukebox played old, cheery music that didn't seem to ever end. It was hit after hit of oldies.

"Well, it looks as though your friend is kicked out. He's been evicted from his place by the landlord," Vincent said to Deon.

"Not good," said Deon shaking his head. He continued with sympathy towards the old man, "I think we have nothing more to gain from this homeless man. Let's call this whole thing off, Vincent. Deal is over. Thank you for your service, brother."

Jasper threw air a few years back, and skipped town shortly after. Throwing air was pool talk for betting without the money to back it up. Deon's debt collector didn't have it easy trying to get the money for Deon. If Vincent was a hit man, things would have been different. Deon didn't like murder, though. He just wanted the money... until now.

When a player loses a bet, a player should pay the debt or suffer the consequences. However, now, they had both admitted it simply wasn't worth fighting for at this point: the money. They legitimately gave up their war with the old man and conceded their efforts out of respect for the old man's misfortunes of late. They didn't want to trouble the old man. Deon also had a big heart for homeless people, and from here on out, he would always be an advocate for the small man in life. Taking the high road felt like the right thing to do. Jasper had thrown air, and everybody knew it. Deon said cheers and held up his glass as it clashed with Vincent's.

Jasper Slovansky was now homeless, but he wasn't giving up. His hustles and side games had only taken him so far. At least he still had his vehicle and knew where he could find help. The only place where he felt he could find redemption was at Kenny's Bar and Grill, where Val was sure to be hanging out. He had heard Val was playing a lot of pool out of Kenny's and doing very well. Maybe they could work something out. The pool room stayed open twenty-four hours a day, seven days a week. Jasper was going to have to sort of thrust his way through the real world for a while until he could get back on his feet and into another apartment or place of residence. The winter snow had settled into the grass and accumulated rather quickly. It was January 2020, and Jasper had realized he needed to start looking out for himself more, and maybe Val could help him do that. Maybe. Maybe not. But either way, Jasper felt like this route was his only hope. So, as he drove he admired the snow and how simply beautiful it looked the way it piled up in sections of mounds from the effects of the snowplows. He observed the snow-covered trees and rooftops. It was a relatively comfortable day, in terms of the weather. Jasper pulled up to the pool room. It was the middle of the day, but there were still a few cars parked outside the room.

Jasper exited the vehicle and walked up the ramp approaching the glass door entrance to Kenny's. Inside the room, he lit a cigarette, but before long somebody from the service desk came up to him and told him to take it outside. Jasper nodded and obediently put the cigarette out. Kenny's had gone non-smoking. The last time Jasper had been in there, everyone smoked and you could barely see across the other end of the room.

He didn't go outside to smoke, because inside the room he saw the man, the one and only Deon Williams. Without anything but sixty dollars on him, Jasper started to walk up to Deon who was sitting down talking with a few friends at the table facing one of the TVs. Deon didn't notice Jasper yet, but Jasper felt as though Deon knew he was there, and felt his presence somehow, or could possibly see him in his peripherals. Jasper suddenly stopped before he got too close to Deon and turned away walking around the pool room casually. He didn't want to engage Deon or anyone yet. Jasper caressed with his finger tips one of the Valley bar tables and took one of the cue balls and finger-flicked it three rails and into the corner pocket. His cue was resting easy in his vehicle. After time went by, thirty minutes or so, he grabbed a bar cue off the wall, and found his "mark" amid a group of junkies in the corner pool table area.

When you find out your deceased father is a legend of the game and a hero in the billiards community, you have to be a bit over-whelmed. That was how Val was feeling on and off. It was af-fecting his pool game a little bit here and there, too. Not to men-tion, Val was hungry to be recognized as the son of the great Louie Roberts. However, he didn't want it to just happen like that. He wanted to earn it, and he knew it wouldn't happen overnight. There were only a few people who knew him as Louie's son, and his sponsor was one of them. Shooter Eddie had marked his cue with Louie's name on it. Val had to tell him the truth, of course.

So, as he drove in his vehicle, he pondered these things and pool. The night sky came quickly. He went about 10 over down the highway in the speeding lane. He considered how he would exact his revenge on Andrew, among other things, as he sped down Highway 270 on his way back home. Suddenly, his phone rang, and he picked it up. It was his sponsor, Shooter.

"Hello?"

"Val? How are you this evening?"

"I'm good, what's the word, boss?"

"I need you to listen. You're a great 9-ball player. But, ehhhh, I noticed something about your game."

"Okay, what's that?"

"You could really use more defensive plays... I mean, your run-out abilities are great! But what about the safety game, man? I'm sure you've heard this before, but you know, isn't the best of-fense a good defense? All I'm saying is... okay, you're not a one-pocket player, are you, Val?"

"Nope... I ..." Val replied and continued to talk back until Shooter interjected.

"I'm assigning you a task, Val. Learn one pocket. You'll be hearing from a pool player soon. I already talked to him and he's going to hook you up with someone big in the scene. He's a world class one pocket player. He's known to be able to give up the world, so I think you could learn a thing or two from him."

Val knew this kind of pool talk pretty well. When Shooter said that he was giving up the world, that meant that the ball spot was probably ridiculously high, meaning he was at a severe disadvantage. In the pool world, when a player is so good, he is asked by his opponents for a ball spot, or handicap, to make the game more fair.

Val was actually pretty excited and eager to learn more about one pocket through the player that Shooter had described to him on the phone. He sped up in his car a little as Shooter described this player, hearing him brag about him. Shooter claimed that his new mentor wanted him to be fresh and not expect too much yet. It would be better to keep his name a mystery at this point, and just let him ease into it. He would be getting lessons in the arts of one pocket, Shooter assured him.

"Val, your pool game is just like your father's, only you're going to be a hell of a one hole player."

It was now Friday, and Val was out and about again, this time at Kenny's Bar and Grill. Kenny's had a big, nine-foot Diamond table with a big screen TV hung on the wall next to it, and a small service bar near the foot of the table where players could grab drinks and order food. A pool table was hung behind the TV screen for flair and pizzazz. The elegance matched with the kid-friendliness of the multi-colored checkered floor of Kenny's attracted a wide batch of people, from country folk to pool players and from drinkers to party-goers. Kenny's was the place to be in Barnhart, MO for a lot of people.

Val got in stroke on the big Diamond table that evening. The energy level of the room remained subdued since the morning, but it was just the calm before the storm. Fridays were always jam-packed with players.

A Diamond table is the pinnacle of tables. It incorporates various billiards elements in each game played with expert craftsmanship and high standards. Diamond tables are made by the players, for the players. Val was usually able to play at his highest gear on Diamonds. Diamonds suited him well. He got warmed up that night while he waited for his new mentor to arrive.

A man named Spider had called him the other night to let him know where and when to be, per instructed by his sponsor, Shooter. Val was to be at Kenny's on Friday night, and nothing else, nothing more. Spider, as guided by Shooter, was setting him up with a mentor, a player that was going to teach him the ropes of one pocket. Val rested his right arm against the bar near the big table and raised his left hand, signaling the waiter. His name was John. He asked John for a Pepsi, and John obliged him.

As he sipped on his drink near the Diamond table, a stranger approached him from out of nowhere. He was an older man. This man had a Cardinals hat on backwards, and the cocky expression on his pale face nearly knocked Val over on his side.

"Well, are ya winning there, ol' big timer?" he asked Val sarcastically, knowing full well that he wasn't playing anyone but himself.

Val looked pretty caught off guard as the man continued talking to him. A few of his buddies were behind him, watching as he talked.

"Hey, I don't mean to be rude, but my name's Andrew," he said and extended a handshake.

"I'm Val. Val Madonna."

"So anyway, you want to play some, maybe some 9-ball?" Andrew asked, as he glared at the cue Val clutched in his hand.

Andrew clearly was looking at the wording etched on the cue, that read, "Louie Roberts." Val knew this wasn't his new mentor the moment he laid eyes on him, but when he had mentioned playing 9-ball, he knew for a fact that something was fishy here. Val laid his cue gently on the table, and stared down his newfound opponent. Andrew stared right back at him, unflinchingly. Neither one of them showing nerves or signs of faltering, they stared through each other's souls. They both knew each other, but not directly. It was only by affiliation and word of mouth. They became acquainted in a matter of seconds. It was incredible, really, how fast they suddenly knew one another, and yet, they had only just met.

"I'll play a little 9-ball, sure!" Val said.

"We'll play some heads-up, then. Okay. You can have the first break."

"Let's do twentey a game. Deal?" Andrew stated and asked him.

Val, trying to dictate the rules, replied.

"Rack your own, and winner breaks?"

Andrew shot Val a snarky look but nodded. Val and Andrew seemed like they were in agreement for the most part.

Val was already warmed up and ready to toast this player for good. Val tried to maintain his composure, and he did a superb job of it, too. Andrew didn't suspect anything, but Val knew who he was. Val knew Andrew as his father's killer. Revenge on the pool table wouldn't be exactly an eye for an eye, but it would suffice.

He broke up the balls, making the wing ball and the 1-ball in the side pocket. He made two balls on the break and had a pretty good opportunity to run out from there. Running out on the first break would be stunning to his newfound adversary, but Val had other plans and was looking to score some. He wanted to first check out how Andrew played. If he moved too quickly on Andrew, he might lose his interest. Val was going to slow play the game. He played a safety on the 5-ball. Three balls remained on the table.

The game went back and forth a lot, just as Val wanted it, too. Eventually Val asked Andrew if he wanted to pump the bet, and Andrew smiled and agreed. They raised the bet to fifty dollars a game, which was a little bit wild considering they just met and the original bet was only twenty a game. Most players don't pump bets to more than double, but there was more to this bet than most bets. This was more about settling a score than anything else. But not the kind of score for money. This was more personal than that. Val wanted to not just take his money, but literally embarrass him, punish him for what he had done to his father.

Now that the bet was pumped up to fifty a rack, Val was content to start playing at his highest level. He kept making ball after ball, running out and never missing a ball. Val was up 400 dollars on Andrew.

"You call this competition?" Andrew yelled.

"No, I call it stealing," Val retorted.

Andrew and his buddies behind him were not smiling. There were fewer of them watching Andrew now than when Andrew first walked in. This was humiliating for them, too.

Val wasn't smiling either, though. He was too focused on continuing his run-outs. His focus and attention on the game was truly incredible and a pure wonder to observe. Val never hesitated and made his runs, pure and simple. Val averted his eyes from the cue ball to the object ball on each shot he made in laser-sharp focus. Repeat. Repeat. He kept going until eventually he had Andrew stuck at 600 dollars. Andrew looked infuriated. Andrew walked over to the table before Val could shoot his last 9-ball.

"Kid, I'm busted. You busted me," Andrew said, and threw down the cash, all of it.

Val got 100 percent of the money and had successfully hustled him out of it. Feeling no guilt, zero, he grabbed the billfolds off the table, twenty-dollar bills along with a few Benjamins, and counted each one. It added up to exactly 650 dollars. The score had been settled. Andrew said he was finished. The game had been played without flaw. Val hustled him on his own, and was proud of himself for it.

The night dragged on, when finally another player approached Val. He was short, with sort of brownish-blonde hair. He wore a Nike T-shirt, with the Just Do It slogan on it. He had a very nice

JB cue case, and he laid it on the table in front of Val before he said anything.

"I'm Justin Bergman. You ready to play some one pocket?" he asked.

"I sure am, but take it easy on me, alright? I've got a family," Val replied, grinning.

Justin racked up all fifteen balls and broke them up.

At the counter facing the nine-foot table, Val noticed an older man sitting down, observing. He was watching Val's last few run-outs when he was playing Andrew. Val had been so focused on beating Andrew that he hadn't even noticed his old mentor who he barely recognized. His hair was now white and his skin more wrinkly than when they had first met. Jasper, not wanting to disturb him any, got up out of his chair and left the pool room with more money than he had when he first walked in. Val smiled for his old mentor as he got down on the cue ball.

A Question and Answer Session with Mark Obrien, Dwayne Spears and Professional Pool Player Justin Bergman on Saint Louie Louie Roberts

Louie Roberts, as described briefly in my book, was a very popular and charismatic pool player back in the 1970s up until his passing. Part of my book is dedicated to Louie and has some subtle references to his life as a professional pool player. So I decided to include a section for just him.

I took the time to ask Mark a few questions to learn more about Louie and the pool scene back in the day. Mark will be the author of a very interesting piece on the complete life of Louie Roberts including many memorable road stories. Mark said he first met Louie at Arway Billiards in 1971.

Mark, how close were you to Louie?

Pretty close, we had a few road trips together.

What was your overall impression of Louie?

He was the most charismatic pool player of all time.

What was Louie's best pool game or hustle?

Beating the ghost in 9-ball. 9-ball was easily his best game.

What was Louie's favorite pool room?

Any and all. He was the center of attention no matter where he went.

What was Louie's dream?

To be the best player on earth.

I heard Louie had a talent for impersonations. Could you tell me what his best one was and who?

Scarface, Al Pacino

Who was the best player Louie ever beat?

Mike Sigel

Dwayne Spears, also a beloved friend of the pool community, took the time to answer some of my questions as well.

When did you first see or meet Louie?

I think I was about eighteen years old, so that would be forty-eight years ago. My dad introduced me to him. It wasn't like meeting a celebrity but just another pool player. My dad took Louie on one of his first road trips. We were at Affton Billiards then owned by Tim Timmerman. By the way, Tim opened up tournament Billiards on Telegraph which later became ride the rail.

Did you ever witness Louie gambling?

Too many times to mention, it was always a joy to watch and listen to him as he played. He would put on a show while playing. So very funny. He had more lines than Ameren Electric. Louie could walk in a pool room cold and play a Road player and the backers would fight over getting in on the action.

Did Louie have any other talents?

He loved movies and did quotes and imitations of different movies and actors and he was also a good gymnast.

How did Louie impress you most as a pool player?

He would just put you in a hypnotic trance watching him play. So fluent and always putting you in awe with the amazing shot-making abilities. Unafraid of any opponent or any shot. His cutting of balls were unequaled to anyone in the game.

I also took the time to hear from pro pool player Justin Bergman about the direction of modern-day pool and on how pool has changed over the years.

Who was the biggest inspiration to your game growing up?

Yeah, I think it's very important to have someone you look up to. When I was younger my favorite players were: Efren Reyes, Earl Strickland, Alex Pagulayan, and Dennis Orcollo.

Where do you think pool is headed as a sport? Will it ever be televised again?

Pool used to be on TV a lot in the 60's, 70's, 80's, then it wasn't for years then it came back on for a few years about ten years ago. Pool is really popular overseas: China, the Philippines, and Taiwan are the biggest three... The Mosconi Cup is on live TV watched by millions all over Europe, even South America but not in the USA. Matchroom just bought the rights to the US Open, so yes, for sure, pool will be on TV again.

What is your impression of Louie? Do you think you could have beaten him if he was alive today?

I never got to meet Louie but heard a lot of stories about him. I think today's players are way ahead of the players ten, twenty years ago. It's not even close. Today's players are levels above than players of the 80's and 90's. And right now I would say there are 100-300 players that play Louie Roberts' level or better.

Joe Evola is an active pool player. Joe grew up in Saint Louis, Missouri and has been playing pool his whole life. He has competed in various pool leagues throughout his career as well. He is the winner of the Missouri 8-ball All Star tournament at Kenny's Bar and Grill in 2017. Joe finished 16th-17th in the US Amateur Pool Championship in 2018 and placed 13th through 16th out of 159 players in the Midwest 9-ball Tour in November, 2019. Joe competes and wins in many small local tournaments as well. Joe also enjoys writing about pool and playing matches on stream at various venues. He's been researching the history of pool and working diligently to become an expert on pool hall drama and other elements of pool for years. He has his own YouTube Channel called Fast Joey's Billiards and you can find Joe on the Social Network as Fast Joey.

Made in the USA
Lexington, KY
10 December 2019

58385313R00090